"YOU DIDN'T WANT
TO GET INVOLVED,"

she said flatly. "That's it, isn't it?"

He wouldn't look at her. "Yes," he admitted finally, his voice low.

"And now?" She had the feeling that disaster was coming, and she wished futilely that she'd never agreed to this conversation. But there was no turning back now; they had to finish it one way or the other. She had to know. "Answer me, Jordan!" she said sharply.

"I don't know," he said. "I just don't know."

Dear Reader,

When two people fall in love, the world is suddenly new and exciting, and it's that same excitement we bring to you in Silhouette Intimate Moments. These are stories with scope, with grandeur. These characters lead the lives we all dream of, and everything they do reflects the wonder of being in love.

Longer and more sensuous than most romances, Silhouette Intimate Moments novels take you away from everyday life and let you share the magic of love. Adventure, glamour, drama, even suspense— these are the passwords that let you into a world where love has a power beyond the ordinary, where the best authors in the field today create stories of love and commitment that will stay with you always.

In coming months look for novels by your favorite authors: Maura Seger, Parris Afton Bonds, Elizabeth Lowell and Erin St. Claire, to name just a few. And whenever you buy books, look for all the Silhouette Intimate Moments, love stories *for* today's women *by* today's women.

Leslie J. Wainger
Senior Editor
Silhouette Books

IMRL-7/85

Foolish Pride

April Thorne

Silhouette Intimate Moments

Published by Silhouette Books New York

America's Publisher of Contemporary Romance

SILHOUETTE BOOKS
300 E. 42nd St., New York, N.Y. 10017

ISBN: 0-373-07106-X

First Silhouette Books printing August, 1985

10 9 8 7 6 5 4 3 2 1

April Thorne dreamed of becoming a writer, but became a medical technician instead. After ten years she took a creative writing course, at her husband's insistence, and has never looked back. The problem now, her husband jokes, is talking her into leaving the typewriter long enough to pay attention to him!

Chapter 1

KENDALL VOSS WAS ON HER KNEES IN THE BARN WHEN she heard the scrunch of tires on the gravel driveway outside. Sitting back on her heels, she uttered a sound of exasperation and pushed her hair out of her eyes with the back of one hand. She held a huge wrench in the other hand, and she threw it down in disgust as she heard a car door slam and then the approach of footsteps.

She wasn't in the mood for company, not after the morning she'd had. Something had spooked the yearlings in the pasture last night; they had run through one of the fences, and by the time she had gotten them corralled again, she'd been exhausted—and sure that they'd done some horrible damage to themselves. Fortunately there had only been cuts and scrapes, nothing serious enough to call the vet about, but she

7

had been applying salve to the worst of them when she noticed to her horror that she was standing in water. When she finally tracked the flood to its source in the barn, the main pipe was spraying a fountain of water in the air, threatening to burst the fitting entirely. The only wrench she could find in a hurry was this gargantuan thing, and every time she tried to tighten the connection, the wrench slipped.

So by the time she heard the car, she was nearly in tears from sheer frustration, and ready to beat the pipe to death in a fit of temper. She didn't want to see anyone in this state; she was dirty and wet and too furious to be civil, even if it was a prospective client. She didn't care right now if the visitor had a hundred horses to board. In fact, if someone gave her a nickel, she'd sell the whole place without a second thought.

"Kendall Voss?"

The voice was masculine, deep and resonant, hiding a trace of amusement. Well aware of the picture she made, with her hair plastered to her face, her blouse untucked and her jeans and boots streaked with mud and water from the blasted pipe, Kendall turned her head.

For an instant, she couldn't say anything. She just sat there on her muddy heels, staring and looking like an idiot. He was the most handsome man she had seen in a long time: dressed in a suit with a white shirt that set off his tanned face, his black hair curled slightly about his ears and just over his collar. His eyes were so dark they seemed as black as his hair, and his mouth could only be called . . . sensual.

But the mouth was curved now into an amused smile, and Kendall realized that she'd been staring. Her face reddening, she jumped up hastily, nearly tripping over her own feet, and felt the flush become crimson. Because she was embarrassed and disconcerted and annoyed by that smile that had now reached the man's dark eyes, she said stiffly, "Yes, I'm Kendall Voss."

He held out his hand. "Jordan Craig. I understand you board horses here."

She was about to hold out her own hand when she realized that her palm was streaked with dirt and greasy from the pipe. Feeling more than ever like a fool, she wiped it down the side of her jeans, trying not to reveal how awkward she felt. Behind her, the sound of escaping water seemed louder, more ominous. She didn't dare turn her head to look; she was afraid of what she would see.

"Maybe I should come back later," Jordan Craig said. "I think I've caught you at a bad time."

A bad time? No, she always looked like this. Feeling increasingly embarrassed, Kendall just wanted him to go away before the pipe burst completely and she had an even bigger mess on her hands. She remembered how the heavy gold ring he wore had flashed when he offered to shake hands, and she decided that she didn't like this man at all—not his obviously tailored city clothes, or his ring, or the smile on his handsome face. How dare he laugh at her! she thought angrily. The least he could do was offer to help.

"There's no reason for you to come back, Mr. Craig," she said flatly. "I can't take any more horses right now."

He looked perplexed. "But I was told that you had facilities here—"

"I'm full up," she said, willing her expression not to reveal the lie, not even sure why she was refusing him. She did have the room; more, she needed the extra income. It was just that he . . . disturbed her. Even through her anger and embarrassment, she realized how attractive he was, how magnetic. There was a compelling quality about his eyes, and she found her own gaze drawn to his again and again. She had to force herself to look away.

She didn't need this, she thought, not after Tony. She was still reeling from her husband's death last year—and from what he had done to her before that. She didn't want to be involved again, and some instinct warned her that that could very easily happen with this man. But she just couldn't handle another relationship, even the chance of one. All her energies were devoted to recovering, emotionally and financially, from the last one. Marrying Tony had been one of the worst mistakes of her life, and the way things were going, she'd be paying for that mistake for a long time.

Then she laughed derisively at herself. What made her think this man might be interested in her? He could probably have any woman he wanted with a mere snap of his fingers. He was obviously successful, obviously financially well-off, if appearance alone was any indication, and he had that indefinable aura of power that was so attractive to so many women. No doubt he had females falling all over themselves, vying for his attention, and in that case, why would he be attracted to her? It was ludicrous, all these absurd thoughts she was entertaining about a man she'd just met. What was the matter with her?

Abruptly, Kendall realized that she'd let the silence go on between them too long. She also realized, a split second before it happened, that she'd ignored the loud hissing from the pipe behind her.

"I'm sorry, Mr. Craig," she said hurriedly. "But I—"

He spoke at the same instant. "Give me the wrench. That pipe looks like—"

It was too late. With a loud pop, the fitting snapped off. Before either of them could move, they were drenched in the ensuing fountain of water. It was like standing under a shower, but worse. The water was icy cold, and the spray so violent that Kendall was almost tumbled off her feet. She stumbled backward, right into him, and felt his hands go around her instinctively, holding her upright.

"The shutoff valve!" he shouted. "Where is it?"

She'd tried to turn it off before, but the thing had been rusted shut and wouldn't budge. "Up there!" she shouted back, gesturing to the coupling eight feet above their heads. "But it won't—"

He didn't debate the issue with her. Grabbing the wrench, he splashed forward and jumped on top of the barrel she had positioned earlier. In seconds, the fountain had eased to a stream, then stopped completely. Thoroughly soaked, they stared at each other in silence.

"I tried to shut it off earlier," Kendall said weakly.

He jumped down from his perch, his face grim. There was a streak of grease across his face, and his immaculate white shirt was sopping, along with the rest of him. Kendall was horrified.

"Your suit!" she cried.

"It'll dry," he said. While she stood there, too mortified to say anything more, he looked down at the pipe. "I'm going to need some fittings and a pipe joint," he said. "And another wrench, if you have one." He looked at her again, that amused smile hovering on his mouth once more. "We might as well fix this now . . . since we're dressed for it."

Kendall found her tongue. "You don't have to . . . I mean, I've caused you enough—"

He wouldn't listen to her protests. In the end, after she gathered most of the things he'd requested, she watched him silently as he worked, and she realized that he was no stranger to tools, despite the suit and the gold ring. He'd taken off his coat and rolled up his wet shirt sleeves, and Kendall was fascinated by his tanned forearms and the play of muscles in his shoulders. She couldn't take her eyes off his hands. They were so capable and sure as he handled the various tools, and once or twice, before she caught herself, she found herself wondering what his hands would feel like on her body. He happened to glance up once at her then, as if he had sensed her thoughts, and she looked away quickly, flushing. She hoped he would finish soon.

"I think that will hold," he said finally, grabbing the rag she held out to him to wipe his hands.

He started to gather the tools he had used, but she said quickly, "Please, leave them. You've done more than enough already. I don't know how to thank you."

He straightened, and she stood with him. "A cup of coffee would be nice," he said, handing the rag back to her.

Their fingers touched as she took the cloth, and Kendall felt a tingle all the way up her arm at the contact. Disconcerted by the sensation, she moved away quickly, leading the way to the house, babbling something about starting the coffee while he washed up in the mud room off the kitchen.

He took her suggestion, and as she went to the sink, she made herself take a deep breath. She started making the coffee, but as she filled the pot with water and added grounds to the basket, her eyes strayed again and again to the closed door of the mud room. She didn't understand what was happening to her. She'd never been so instantly attracted to a man, not even the one she'd married. She had to snap out of it, she told herself fiercely. Jordan Craig was a client, a man who had come here asking about boarding horses. For all she knew, he had a wife and six children and had been ecstatically married for years and years. He had to have been. A man like that wouldn't remain single for long; he would have been snagged long ago.

Maybe she was having all these fantasies because she had been alone at the ranch too long. She couldn't remember the last time she'd gone shopping for anything but groceries and feed, and it had been months since she'd gone out on a date, an experience that had been such a disaster that she didn't care to repeat it.

Dennis Atchison had been a friend of her husband; she hadn't realized that he'd always wanted to be much more than a friend to her. She tried to tell him that night that she wasn't ready for another relationship; the wounds Tony had dealt were still too fresh. What she didn't tell him—although lately she'd been tempted to since he persisted in coming around—was that she didn't want a relationship with him. He was too jealous, too possessive, and that irritated her no end. Especially since he had no right to feel that way in the first place. She wasn't "his girl," despite the fact that he had somehow convinced himself that she was. She wasn't anybody's *girl,* she told herself firmly, and it was going to stay that way.

The mud room door opened just then, and Jordan came into the kitchen, glancing around appreciatively. Kendall followed his glance, trying to see the place through his eyes and thinking that even a stranger had to find it welcoming. It was a big room, as most kitchens are in old Victorian houses: sunny and bright, the hub of the house. When Kendall's father was alive, he'd used the study for his office, but since his death two years before, Kendall had moved the office into an alcove here that had been used for meals. When she sat at her desk, she could look through the windows toward the paddocks and the barn, and she loved that view, just as she loved the house itself, with its old-fashioned high-ceilinged rooms and casement windows. Her grandfather had built the house; Kendall was the third generation to live here, and the thought that she might not be able to keep it haunted her.

"These old houses are really something, aren't they?" Jordan commented as he sat down at the battered old oak table Kendall used for meals.

Kendall brought mugs to the table, self-consciously shoving aside a pile of horse magazines and breeding records that she'd been going through at dinner last night. She hung the halter and lead rope she'd brought in to repair on the back of her chair, noting Jordan's smile as she did so.

"I'm sorry the place is such a mess," she said, embarrassed again. There just wasn't enough time to take care of the house and the horses, too, she thought. She desperately needed help in the barn, but she couldn't afford it. After Tony had died and she found out about the mountain of debts he'd incurred—and that she had inherited—she had had to let their help go. Their salaries hadn't been much, but she needed every penny she could save.

Jordan took a sip of coffee. "Don't apologize," he said. "Houses are supposed to look lived in."

Kendall forced a laugh, too aware of his dark eyes on her. "Well, this one certainly does."

"Do you run this place all by yourself?"

"Doesn't it show?" she answered lightly. Why was he looking at her like that?

He smiled. "Well, it looks like you could use a little help. With the plumbing, at least."

She nodded, acknowledging the remark with a wry grimace, but thinking that she could use help with more than that. The fence the yearlings had trampled last night had to be repaired before the pasture could be used again, and the list of things that had to be mended or replaced seemed to grow daily. Sometimes she felt that if one more thing went wrong, she'd break down completely.

But she wasn't going to admit that, especially to him. She'd managed this long on her own; she'd just have to keep going. Somehow.

"I appreciate your help today," she said. "And since it was my fault, I'd like to pay for your suit. It's the least I can do."

Jordan shook his head. "I'd rather you took my horses for boarding," he said, looking directly at her.

Kendall wanted to glance away from him. She had the absurd feeling that she could be mesmerized by his eyes, that she could fall soundlessly into their deep dark pools and never be herself again. It was a frightening feeling, fascinating and repellent at the same time. With an effort, she wrenched her gaze away and forced herself to take a sip of coffee. To her dismay, her hand shook when she lifted the cup to her lips.

"I know you said you don't have room," Jordan went on, seemingly mercifully oblivious to her state of confusion. "But it would be only temporary. I just bought the Ferguson property, and I'll be building my own place there."

Kendall set her cup down with a thud, staring at him in astonishment. The Ferguson property had been on the market for years, at some astronomical price that was exorbitant even for the Scottsdale area, which was known for its high-priced land. Part of the house had been destroyed by a fire, and the dilapidated barn wasn't in much better condition. The fencing, what was left of it, was falling down, and the land—some forty acres of it—had crept back to its natural state long ago. Kendall couldn't imagine anyone buying the place; the cost of renovation alone was mind-boggling. But the most disturbing thought of all was that the Ferguson property abutted hers. If Jordan Craig was serious— and she didn't doubt that he was—she realized with dismay that they would be neighbors.

"Is something wrong?" Jordan asked, breaking Kendall's stunned silence.

"Wrong?" she stammered. "No, of course not. It's just . . . just that I'm surprised."

"Why?"

"Well, I—" She got up abruptly to pour more coffee, trying to give herself time to frame an appropriate answer. The thought that Jordan was going to be her neighbor was unnerving, and she didn't know why it should be. What difference did it make if he lived next door?

Next door? The Ferguson house was acres away; she couldn't even see it from her place. She and Jordan could live side by side for years and never see each other. What was she worried about?

She wasn't worried; it was a ridiculous thought. If he

wanted to spend his time and money refurbishing that property, it wasn't any business of hers.

"You what?" Jordan asked curiously as she came back to the table.

She shrugged, trying to sound as if she didn't really care. "Well, that property has been for sale for years. I guess we all thought no one was ever going to buy it."

"It's a beautiful piece of land."

She had to agree with that; those forty acres were almost as beautiful as her own property. She ought to know, she thought, since her father had been forced to sell that acreage to Ferguson in the first place, years ago. The money had gone to pay her mother's medical bills, and Aaron Voss had just managed to keep these last ten acres as an inheritance for his daughter. It had been a hard fight for Aaron to save what was left of the ranch for her, and Kendall was determined to see that his sacrifices hadn't been in vain. She loved this place; it was more than a business to her, more even than a home. It was part of her father, and she wouldn't let it go.

"Of course," Jordan went on, "it's going to require a lot of work before it's usable again—both the land and the house. That's why I need someplace to keep the horses."

"Where did you keep them before?"

"I didn't," he confessed. "Mine's a classic case of putting the cart before the horse—or the horse before the barn, I guess. I bought the mares when I was still looking for property."

He looked so abashed that she laughed. "So you haven't owned horses before?" When he shook his head, curiosity got the best of her, and she started to ask, "What made you decide—"

He frowned, and Kendall realized instantly that she had made a mistake. Embarrassed, she said hastily, "I'm sorry. I didn't mean to pry."

Jordan relaxed with a visible effort. "That's all right," he said, although she saw by his expression that it wasn't all right at all. "I just decided that I . . . that I needed a new hobby. Arabian horses seemed to fit the bill."

"I see," Kendall said, suddenly cool. She saw, all right. He was just what she had suspected all along: a wealthy man who had decided to cash in on the current mania of using Arabian horses as tax shelters. People like Jordan didn't care about the animals themselves; the horses were just another number on some corporate tax form. She couldn't understand people like that; she had loved Arabians from the time she was old enough to know what a horse was, and to her they were more than mere animals, or investments. She couldn't help it; she felt only contempt for the owners who couldn't pick their horses out of a group, people who had never done anything more for their animals than write checks for their upkeep, or appear at important shows to clap enthusiastically when their horse won— after it was pointed out to them which one in the show ring it was.

Tony had often criticized her for her attitude. After all, he'd point out, those same investors were the ones who kept Voss Arabians going. Where would Kendall be without people like that to buy the horses she had for sale, or to board those same animals at the ranch for a fee? In her calmer moments, she had to concede his point. But the situation still rankled.

It rankled now. Kendall wanted to refuse to take his horses on sheer principle. But she had the room, and she desperately needed the money. The future of the ranch was too high a price to pay for the sake of pride; and besides, she owed him this after his help this morning. "How many horses are we talking about, Mr. Craig?" she asked finally.

"Jordan, please. And right now, it's only the three mares." He smiled deprecatingly. "At least, that's all the trouble I've managed to get into in such a short time. No doubt later there will be more, but by then I expect to have my own place operational."

She couldn't resist. "How big an operation do you intend to have?"

He shrugged, smiling again. "I'm not sure at this point. I thought I'd take it one step at a time." He hesitated. "I'm not sure I'm doing the right thing, anyway. All those bloodlines and names are so confusing; it's easy to make a mistake. Of course," he added, "not for someone like you. I imagine you know all these mysterious pedigrees by heart."

"I should," Kendall said, trying not to feel flattered. "I've been in the business all my life."

"Well, you obviously have an advantage, then. I had to rely on someone else's advice when I bought these horses. It was a new experience for me, I confess. I'm used to making decisions on an informed basis, not taking a shot in the dark."

She had no doubt that he was accustomed to making decisions, probably important ones. He was obviously a man who was used to running things—undoubtedly his own way. She suspected that it had galled him no end having to rely on someone else's opinion; she just hoped he'd been given good advice. She'd seen so many new owners purchase inferior horses for outrageous prices simply because they didn't know what they were doing. Neophytes in this business were sometimes so dazzled at the prospect of doubling or tripling their money that they didn't realize how many people were forced to sell at a loss because the products of their ill-conceived breeding programs just weren't worth anything. By the time they found out that they'd been given bad advice, it was too late.

Kendall was about to caution Jordan about this unsavory aspect of the horse world, but she held her tongue. It wasn't any of her business what he did with his money, just as it wasn't any concern of hers what kind of horses he had. Maybe if he made a few expensive mistakes, he'd realize that his new "hobby" required a little more thought than writing checks with strings of zeros on them.

She looked at him, pride in her profession warring with this sudden, inexplicable attraction she felt. Reminding herself fiercely that she'd known too many men like him who were only interested in a rapid turnover of horses at a quick profit, she said, "I'll be glad to board your horses, Mr. Craig. Just as long as it's only temporary."

He smiled slightly then, aware of her cool tone and for some reason amused by it. She stood, annoyed because she suspected that he was laughing at her, and he stood with her. To her surprise, she saw that it was difficult for him to get up. A flicker of pain crossed his face as he pulled himself stiffly to his feet, and she was alarmed. Had he hurt himself when he helped her in the barn? Without thinking, she blurted, "Are you all right?"

He looked irritated at the question. "Of course I'm all right. Why?"

There was a challenge in his tone, and she faltered, "You seemed . . ."

He straightened, almost towering over her. She hadn't realized he was so tall; even in her boots, her head was just above his shoulder, and she was five foot seven in her bare feet. He had to be over six feet, she thought, and unconsciously she straightened too. What was it about this man that made her feel so defensive, as if she had to be on her guard against him?

"I'll have the horses transported as soon as possible," he said as he left. "You can call me when they arrive. If that's convenient for you."

She agreed that it was, then stood at the door, watching him walk to his car. She frowned when she saw him limp slightly, as if favoring the right side of his body, and she wondered again if he had injured himself. When he got stiffly into his car—a sleek, midnight blue late-model Lincoln—she frowned again. The car seemed to symbolize the vast difference in their lifestyles, underscoring what she had thought about him before. Was he just a wealthy man dabbling in horses because he was bored? She didn't want to think so; to her dismay, she realized as she closed the door that she wanted him to be much more than that.

Jordan drove slowly away, aware of the throbbing in his back. He must have twisted it somehow when he jumped on that barrel, and he was angry at himself, and at his body for betraying him again. Sometimes he wondered if he would ever fully recover physically from the car accident, but then he thought that maybe it was just punishment. Even after a year, he still felt guilty at the thought of it, but at least he had stopped wishing that he had been the one to die in the wreck, not his wife, Marie. Maybe that was progress of a sort. His friend and financial adviser, Martin Holbrook, said it was, but what did Marty know? *His* wife hadn't died while *he* was at the wheel.

It didn't make any difference that the accident hadn't been his fault. The best driver in the world couldn't have anticipated a drunk running a red light. The irony of it was that the other driver hadn't even been hurt. Of course, Jordan hadn't found that out for days afterward; he hadn't even known Marie had died until he regained consciousness, cemented into a body cast because he had broken his back.

Jordan shook his head to clear it of memories of that terrible time. He still had nightmares about that night, but at least they were fewer now, and farther between. He hoped Marty had been right about this horse business; he needed something to occupy his mind until—if ever—he went back to work. He'd been going crazy sitting around the apartment after selling the house; he just wasn't cut out for idleness.

So he had taken Marty's advice, and now he was involved whether he wanted to be or not. Maybe it *was* a good thing. Buying those horses and negotiating for that property had taken his mind off . . . other things . . . for the first time in months.

Surprised, Jordan realized that Kendall Voss had taken his mind off Marie, too. He smiled, recalling Kendall huddled over that hissing pipe, and he laughed aloud when he remembered the look on her face as it burst. He hadn't felt so alive in a long, long time as he had this morning, repairing that pipe for her.

And he hadn't felt so attracted to another woman since Marie had died. Thinking about Kendall's deli- ~

cate features, her expressive eyes and slender body, Jordan felt something stir inside him, something he had thought had died along with his wife.

Such a fierce, proud woman, he thought, and grinned. Maybe this horse business wouldn't be so bad after all. He would have to find a way to see the independent Miss Voss more often.

On business, of course.

Chapter 2

JORDAN HAD GIVEN KENDALL A PHONE NUMBER WHERE HE could be reached when the horses arrived. The transport company called Friday morning to tell her that the van would be there that day, and as Kendall dialed Jordan's number, she was annoyed at herself for being so nervous. She had to dial the digits twice because her hand shook the first time, and as she listened to the ringing at the other end, she made herself take a deep breath. He was only a man, after all, she told herself, a *client*. It wasn't as if she were calling him for a date; she was just going to tell him that the horses would be here soon. What could be simpler than that?

"Craig."

Kendall wasn't prepared for the abrupt way he answered the phone. Her heart skipped a beat when she heard his voice, and she had to make a conscious effort not to stammer. What was the *matter* with her? Gripping the receiver tightly, she managed to say, "This is Kendall Voss, Mr. Craig. I'm calling to tell you that your horses are supposed to arrive sometime today."

There. That was straightforward enough, she thought. She had even sounded brisk and businesslike herself. He couldn't know that her heart was pounding madly, or that she had to fight the impulse to hang up before she asked when she was going to see him again.

"I'm tied up here for a while," the deep voice said in her ear. "But I'd like to come out and see them later this afternoon, if that's all right with you."

All right with her? She felt like dancing around the kitchen in sheer anticipation. "They're your horses, Mr. Craig."

"Yes, but it's your ranch. I wouldn't want to intrude if you're going to be busy."

"I'm always busy, Mr. Craig. You'll find that out when you have a place of your own."

"Oh, well, if it would be inconvenient . . . ."

Kendall was dismayed. She hadn't meant to imply that he shouldn't come. She said hastily, "It won't be inconvenient at all," and winced when she realized how eager she sounded. "I mean," she added, trying to regain control over her voice, "that I have to be here anyway."

That was even worse. Kendall winced at the coolness in his voice when he said, "I see." She closed her eyes, thinking that now she had offended him. She was furious with herself. She had planned on sounding so poised, so calm and in control, and she had succeeded only in sounding like a complete idiot.

Trying to salvage the situation, she said, "But even if I'm not here, you're welcome to come. I know you must be anxious to see how they withstood the trip."

"Yes," he said again, his voice still cool. "Well, perhaps I'll see you later, then. Thank you for calling."

She hung up the phone, grimacing. She'd certainly made a mess of that, she thought bleakly. What was wrong with her? She'd been dealing with clients all her life—or as long as she could remember, anyway. Why was Jordan Craig so different?

He wasn't different. He just had an uncanny way of making her say the wrong thing. It was infuriating, but she wouldn't make the same mistake again. In the meantime, she had stalls to clean before those horses arrived. If she had to mope around about anything, it ought to be all the chores she still had to do today. Getting all those things done should occupy her mind—and more. She wouldn't have time to think about Jordan, or wonder why she was reduced to stammering idiocy just at the sound of his voice.

Kendall was still in the barn when the huge truck pulled into the yard. When she saw who the driver was, she smiled, waving a welcome, glad it was Dave who had come. She'd known Dave Lindley for years; he'd been a longtime friend of her father, and he was considered one of the most conscientious drivers in the horse-transport business. The Vosses had always requested Dave when they had a horse to transport because, unlike so many others, he would stop every eight hours on a long haul to check his passengers and give them a rest—an important consideration, since a cross-country drive took days. When he saw Kendall wave at him, he grinned back and climbed down out of the cab to give her a hug.

"Haven't seen you for a long time, Sprout," he said, using the nickname he had given her years ago. He held her away from him, his smile fading to a concerned frown. "You look tired, Kendall. Are you feeling all right?"

"Of course I am," she replied, making light of it. "I'm as strong as a horse!"

"You don't look it. You've lost weight again. Maybe this place is too much for you to run by yourself."

"Now don't start that again! We had this same conversation before, remember?"

Dave nodded, and they were both silent a moment, thinking of when that conversation had taken place. It was right after Tony had died, and Kendall had been going through a deep depression, unable to conquer her guilt. The marriage had been in trouble from the start; she hadn't realized until she married him that Tony wasn't the man she'd thought him to be. She had thought that he was willing to work as hard as she to make the ranch a success, but she hadn't found out until too late that Tony's ideas of success were entirely different from hers.

Kendall often thought that she never would have married Tony if her father hadn't died several months before. When she met him, she was still feeling the loss, still adrift. She and Aaron had been partners in Voss Arabians from the time she was in her teens; when she turned eighteen, he had papers drawn up making it official. She'd been so proud that day, and she had vowed never to betray the faith and trust he'd shown in her.

Kendall had always had an eye for horses, and after Aaron officially made her a partner in the business, she worked harder than before, honing that natural talent to a fine edge over the next eight years. Their breeding program flourished, and the stock they sold brought excellent prices. Voss Arabians became even more well known in the Arabian horse world than it had been, and buyers came from all over the country. They were never disappointed.

But Aaron had been worried about his daughter; he had tried to persuade her to go out more, to socialize in other areas that didn't involve horses. He was concerned that love and romance would pass her by; he wanted her to have a little fun.

She should have heeded his advice, Kendall thought, long after Tony's accident. If she had, she would have been more experienced, wiser in the ways of men. She might have seen through Tony then, or at least she wouldn't have been so desperately eager to believe his lies, or to turn a deaf ear to the rumors that began about him so soon after they were married.

He had been such a charmer, that was the problem. He could be so guileless, so *sincere,* even when he was pulling a fast one.

And he'd pulled plenty of those, Kendall thought, cringing at the memory of the deals he'd made behind her back, of the double commissions he'd charged for selling horses, of how he'd cheated buyer and seller alike. He had pocketed all that money, of course, and spent it—thrown it away—at the gambling tables. She never would have found out if one of their customers hadn't mentioned the price he'd paid for a mare that Tony had acted as agent on. The amount was thousands of dollars more than the asking price, so she'd gotten curious enough to call the seller, who told her in surprise that the horse hadn't sold for nearly that much. Sure that there had been some misunderstanding,

Kendall had confronted Tony about it. To her horror, he not only admitted inflating the selling price, he actually was proud that he'd gotten away with it.

Even then, Kendall thought, *even then* she had believed him when he promised he would never do it again. It had taken another irate client, and the threat of a lawsuit for fraud, to make her realize what a blind, stupid little fool she'd been. She and Tony had a serious fight that night, and he was furious when she said he'd had his last chance. She wanted him to get out; she never wanted to see him again.

Her words had been more prophetic than she knew. Tony roared off on the new motorcycle he had just brought home, and he lost control somewhere on a road. Always the daredevil, he wasn't wearing a helmet.

It had taken her a long time, and some painful soul-searching, to rid herself of the crushing weight of guilt and remorse she felt over Tony's death. She tortured herself for weeks afterward, thinking that she was responsible. Then she learned about the huge debts Tony had left behind, and anger took the place of guilt. She was legally responsible for those debts, and in order not to lose the ranch itself, she had to sell off most of their stock just to keep afloat.

But there was one horse she hadn't sold, as bleak as things had been—and still were. Cantata was a direct descendant of the foundation broodmares for Voss Arabians; Kendall would never dream of selling that mare. She had bred her, raised her, and bred her back only to the best, improving the Voss stock with every resulting foal. Cantata was almost twenty years old now, and her life as a brood mare would come to an end in just a few years. But she was in foal now, to a

champion stallion whose stud fee had taken almost
every penny Kendall had left. If the foal was as good as
Kendall hoped it would be, its sale would clear the last
of her debts and give her a chance at a new future.
Everything rested on Cantata and the coming foal. So
much depended on it that sometimes Kendall would
wake up in the middle of the night, wondering what she
would do if something went wrong.

But nothing would go wrong, Kendall told herself
fiercely, again and again. The foal would be perfect, the
best Voss Arabians had yet produced. It would save the
ranch—and Kendall's own future, too. It had to; she
had nothing else to count on.

"Well, let's get these mares unloaded," Dave said,
interrupting Kendall's thoughts. "I've got to finish this
run to Los Angeles, but I might be persuaded to take
time for a cup of coffee if I'm invited."

Kendall grinned at him. "You're always invited; you
know that. And in your honor I've already made some
of that horrible black brew you call coffee. I imagine
it's probably standing up by itself by now!"

"Just the way I like it," Dave said, unperturbed.
"How do you think I stay awake on these long hauls,
anyway?"

Kendall was surprised when they unloaded the first
of Jordan's horses; she was astonished at the second,
and by the time the third stepped out of the van, she
was frankly nonplussed. Gazing at the three mares with
a practiced eye, she thought that whoever had acted as
his agent on this package certainly knew what he was
doing. Each one was better than the last, and excellent
breeding was evident in every fine line, each delicate
flare of a nostril, every bright eye. They were an

outstanding group, and Kendall was annoyed to realize that she couldn't have done better herself. As she helped Dave put them in the three stalls she had cleaned that morning, she couldn't help wishing that Jordan had made some expensive mistakes with these horses. It would have served him right, she thought, dilettante that he was. Then she was ashamed of herself. She was just angry because she had been mistaken about him—for the second time. As much as it galled her to admit that, it was true.

It was even more galling to realize that she hadn't been able to get him out of her mind. For the past three days it seemed that she'd done nothing but think about him. Images would pop into her mind when she was going over the bills, or feeding the horses, or repairing the fences. She'd remember the way he walked, the gestures he made with his hands, how black his hair was. She'd see him bending over that broken pipe, frowning in concentration; she'd picture him drinking coffee at the kitchen table.

But most of all, she thought irritably, she'd remember his amused smile. The more she thought about that, the more annoyed she became. He had been laughing at her the entire time, and it irked her that she was the focus of some private, internal joke. *That* was why she had hoped he had made some expensive mistakes with these mares; it would have been sweet revenge for his superior attitude.

Dave was just leaving when Kendall heard the car in the driveway. She turned to see who it was, annoyed to realize that she hoped the visitor would be Jordan, and disgusted at the quick leap of her heart at the thought of seeing him again. But when she recognized the battered orange truck belonging to Dennis Atchison, her mouth tightened, and she frowned as he pulled up in a spray of gravel and jumped out.

"I was on my way into town and I thought I'd stop by and see if you wanted to come with me," Dennis said cheerfully, ignoring Kendall's black expression. "We could get a drink or something, whatever you like."

"It's the middle of the day, Dennis," she said, her voice flat.

He wasn't put off by her tone. "Well, how about lunch, then?"

"I've already had lunch," she answered, starting to walk away. "I've got work to do."

He followed her, a slight man her own age, with sandy hair and light blue eyes and freckles. She hated freckles on a man, she thought irritably, and tried to ignore him, hoping he'd get the hint and leave.

He didn't; he never did. After their first and only disastrous date, Kendall had tried to tell him gently that she just wasn't interested. For some obtuse reason, he had refused to believe her. He called constantly and stopped by every few days, persisting in his maddening fantasy that she was just playing hard to get. She'd given up trying to be polite, but it seemed that overt rudeness wasn't working either. When he followed her into the barn, she lost what was left of her patience. Turning to face him, she said, "I told you I had work to do, Dennis. Now, if you don't mind—"

"Why don't I give you a hand?"

The man was oblivious, absolutely oblivious! Kendall thought, exasperated. But short of throwing him off the place bodily, there wasn't much she could do. She tried again. "Look, Dennis—"

"Hey! Where'd you get these horses?" he asked

suddenly, walking toward the first of the three stalls. "Are they yours?"

She wished they were. She'd give her right arm just to have one of them, she thought. Gritting her teeth, she answered nastily, "Of course they're not mine! They belong to a new client."

"Oh—who?"

"His name is Jordan Craig," she answered curtly, not wanting to discuss it.

"Jordan Craig?" Dennis whistled. "I've heard about him."

Kendall had been about to insist that he leave. Now, of course, she had to find out what he meant. "What do you mean, you've heard about him?" she asked suspiciously.

Dennis leaned nonchalantly against the stall, clearly enjoying the idea that he had her attention for once. "Oh," he said. "Things."

"What things?" she demanded. "Listen, Dennis—if there's something I should know about him, you'd better tell me. I don't want to be responsible for his horses if there's going to be trouble."

"Well, that depends on what you mean by trouble."

In another minute she'd strangle him with her bare hands. Trying to control herself, she said, "Tell me what *you* mean."

"All right, all right. You're going to find out anyway."

"Find out what?"

"I heard he bought the Ferguson place—"

"That's not news," she scoffed. "He told me that himself."

"Yeah, but did he tell you what he plans to do with it?"

"He's going to build a ranch," she said contemptuously. "So what?"

"Not just a ranch," Dennis said. "A showplace. Bigger than Kaylene's, from what I heard. The guy's loaded, Kendall," he added. "The rumor is that he wants to buy your property, too."

Kendall stared at him, not sure whether to believe him or not. She knew how jealous Dennis was, how possessive, even when he had no right to be. He could be fabricating the whole thing just to rattle her—to make sure that she would consider Jordan an enemy instead of the attractive man he was. She wouldn't put it past Dennis to try that; he'd done similar things before. He'd tried to drive a wedge between her and Tony, she recalled—and Tony had been his best friend at the time. The fact that she wished now that he had succeeded was beside the point.

"He's got forty acres, Dennis," she said finally. "Why would he want more?"

He looked at her pityingly. "Why do you think? If he owned this piece, he'd have the whole road frontage. No one would have to drive by your place to get to his. He'd have the only ranch out here—no distractions to potential buyers. It makes sense, doesn't it?"

Unfortunately, it did. Kendall finally got rid of Dennis, but not before she told him in no uncertain terms to stay out of her life. If only he'd do as she said! Then she sat on a bale of hay and contemplated what he had told her, still wondering whether to believe him or not.

If Jordan had an eye on her property, he wouldn't be the first, she thought. Other people had approached her with offers—initially when her father died, and then again after Tony's death. She had haughtily refused them all.

Maybe Jordan knew that, she thought suddenly. If he was half the businessman she suspected he was, it wouldn't have been difficult for him to find out how precarious her financial status was. She knew that powerful men like Jordan Craig had ways of finding out anything they wanted; it was why they were so successful. So if he had discovered her desperate straits, he would also know that she had stubbornly refused all those other offers. Thoughtfully, she looked at the three mares contentedly munching the hay she had given them. An ugly suspicion formed in her mind, and she frowned. It hadn't occurred to her before, but what better way for Jordan to get past her defenses than with horses?

The more she thought about it, the more sense it made. Why else would he have asked to board his horses here when there were far more luxurious places to keep them in this area?

Van Zandt Farms was one, Kendall thought darkly, remembering that Dennis had mentioned Jordan's plans to have an even grander place than Kaylene's. But if that was true, he had his work cut out for him. Kaylene Van Zandt was one of the wealthiest women in Scottsdale—probably in the whole state, Kendall admitted, her mouth tight. She should be; she'd been married five times, each to a man richer than the one before. In her sixties now, Kaylene seemed to be concentrating more on her horses than in acquiring any new husbands. Her ranch was indeed a showplace—or at least some people thought it was. Kendall thought it garish and ostentatious and beyond belief, all the barns having been constructed at great cost to resemble huge tents, complete with copper roofs.

Maybe she was just prejudiced. She had never gotten along with Kaylene; even her father had had his differences with her, because Kaylene was jealous of their success. Kendall had inherited the feud, which had intensified this past year when Kaylene offered to buy Cantata and Kendall laughed in her face. She knew why Kaylene coveted that mare—if she owned Cantata, the last of the foundation stock for Voss Arabians, it would mean that she had triumphed over her old enemy. Kendall was determined that Kaylene would never know the taste of that particular victory, even if Kendall lost everything else.

"You look deep in thought," a now-familiar voice said behind her.

Startled, Kendall sprang up from the hay bale. She'd been so preoccupied that she hadn't heard him drive in; for a second or two she just stared blankly at him, unprepared. Jordan didn't look like the same man who had visited earlier in the week; the suit and tie were gone, and he was wearing a plaid sport shirt and jeans instead. To her surprise, he was also wearing running shoes, and she gave him a point for that. She'd seen so many new horse owners swaggering around with un-creased Stetsons, hand-tooled belts with huge silver buckles and boots that had obviously just been bought —as if the outfit alone could make them the horsemen they were pretending to be. She was always secretly amused at such pretensions, especially when she casual-ly handed one of them a lead rope. If the other end of the line was attached to a horse, the would-be horse-man quickly became a city slicker again, ridding himself of the rope as rapidly as possible, usually by literally throwing it back at her. Kendall doubted somehow that Jordan Craig fit into this private category of hers; he seemed capable of anything. And probably was, she thought grimly.

"Do I pass?" he asked.

Kendall flushed, realizing belatedly that she had been staring. He was smiling that amused smile of his, and she immediately became annoyed. "I'm sorry," she said. "I was . . . thinking."

"Then I'm sorry too. I didn't mean to interrupt."

"It wasn't important."

"I see."

He sounded amused again, and Kendall turned abruptly away, wondering why he always made her feel so incredibly inept. Picking up a halter, she said, "Your mares arrived a couple of hours ago. They're over here."

Seemingly unperturbed by her abruptness, Jordan fell into step beside her. As they approached the first stall, he said casually, "I brought their pedigrees with me, if you'd like to see them."

She didn't need to see their pedigrees; she already knew that all three came from top bloodlines. But because she detected something behind that deliberately casual tone, she glanced at him. He didn't look amused now; he seemed intent on her reply. Almost as if, she thought in surprise, he really wanted her opinion. Their eyes met, and despite herself, Kendall felt something stir inside her. He was so handsome, she thought confusedly. Why did he have to be so good-looking?

She deliberately looked away. Her experience with Tony should have taught her that a man's physical appearance was no guarantee of character. Tony had been tall and handsome too, she reminded herself, and she had been too blinded by his looks to see the slyness in his eyes. She wasn't going to make the same mistake with Jordan, she vowed, especially not after what she'd heard today. Oh, no; this time she would be on her guard.

"I'd like to see their papers," she heard herself say, and was appalled. She hadn't meant to say that; she wanted him to look at his horses and then leave before she betrayed herself.

Betrayed herself! But there was nothing to hide! Hadn't she just decided that Jordan was a client and nothing more?

Seemingly unaware of Kendall's tumult of emotion, Jordan paused at the first stall. "What do you think?" he asked, turning to look at her with those dark eyes.

Kendall looked down at the halter she was carrying, thinking bemusedly that she didn't know what to think at all. What was happening to her? One minute she wanted him to leave; the next she was hoping that she could convince him to stay.

"I think you've bought yourself some excellent horses," she said finally, trying to sound calm and matter-of-fact when she felt so much the opposite.

He smiled at that, genuinely pleased. "Then you think they'll be a start for a breeding program?"

"You could breed these mares to any top stallion in the country and get a wonderful foal crop," she answered honestly.

"But you haven't seen the pedigrees yet. How can you be sure?"

"Because I know horses," she said simply. "And all anyone has to do is look at them to know how good they are."

He nodded, reaching out to pat the mare's neck. "I thought so," he murmured. "But I wanted to be sure."

"I don't know who advised you on buying these three, but whoever it was, you'd better put them on retainer. They obviously knew what they were doing."

He smiled again, leaning sideways against the stall door to gaze down at her. "You really think so?"

"Yes," she answered, surprised and a little annoyed at the question.

He pushed himself away from the stall, holding her eyes. She could see the laughter in the depths of his, and she stiffened, wondering what the joke was.

"I'm glad to hear you say that," he said. "Because I selected them myself."

"You!"

"You sound surprised."

"I am," she blurted without thinking. Then, aware of his quick grin, she added accusingly, "You said you didn't know anything about horses!"

"Let's just say I'm learning." He looked beyond her then, exclaiming, "Is that one of yours?"

Diverted, Kendall looked around, and she laughed when she saw Cantata at her stall door, nodding her head up and down, trying to get their attention. "Yes, she's mine," she said, unable to keep the note of pride from her voice. She followed Jordan across the aisle. "Her name is Cantata."

"She's . . . beautiful," Jordan said admiringly.

Kendall scratched the silver gray mare between the ears, agreeing wholeheartedly with Jordan's assessment. Even though Cantata was now almost twenty years old, she still had that undefined and so desirable quality that horsemen called presence. Her huge dark eyes were kind, almost wise, and her finely etched head with its prominent tear bones and teacup muzzle was a classic. She was the finest horse, mare or stallion, that Kendall had ever owned, a truly elegant representative of the Arabian breed. And as Cantata butted her head against Kendall's shoulder, Kendall thought fiercely to herself that she would die before giving her up. Cantata had several more years yet before she stopped producing because of her age, but her value to Kendall went far beyond that. She didn't care how sentimental it sounded; she loved this horse. And she would do anything to keep her.

"And you say *I* have some fine mares," Jordan said after a while.

Kendall smiled. "Well, I have to admit, this one is pretty special. And if the foal she's carrying is half as good as she is—" She stopped abruptly. She wasn't going to confess just how much the coming foal meant to her, especially to Jordan.

If he noticed her hesitation, he didn't comment on it. Instead he asked casually, "Who's she in foal to?"

"A stallion called Ibn Al Zahr," Kendall answered, relieved that he hadn't pursued the subject. "He's—"

"I know—the national champion from a few years back."

Kendall was surprised that he knew. But she shouldn't have been, she told herself in sudden annoyance; the man seemed full of surprises. "Yes," she said abruptly, giving Cantata a final pat. Then, casually, "I hope the foal will live up to its breeding."

"That shouldn't be a problem—not with a mare like that."

As they walked out of the barn again, Kendall couldn't help noticing the way Jordan casually looked around. As she followed the direction of his glance, she

winced inside. Even to her eyes the place was starting
to look shabby. Weeds were encroaching on the driveway, and all the fences needed repainting. She sighed
heavily. She just couldn't do it all by herself; the horses
alone took all her time, and maintainance work—
except for the most immediate repairs—just had to
wait.

Stifling the urge to apologize for the way the place
looked, Kendall said instead, "I'm sure the mares will
settle in all right, but if there are any problems, I'll let
you know."

Jordan looked at her again, studying her for a minute
before he smiled. "I hope so."

Kendall flushed, wondering why she had said such a
stupid thing. *Of course* she would call him if anything
went wrong, she berated herself angrily. No wonder he
was laughing at her. Feeling like a fool, she said
awkwardly, "Well, I've got to get back to work."

"Is that all you do—work?"

Without thinking, she made a face. "It seems so. But
I'm sure you'll find the same thing when you start
construction on your place. There are always a thousand and one details to see to, don't you think?"

"I'm finding that out. I moved into the house—or
what was left of it—yesterday."

She stared at him. "So soon?"

"You sound dismayed. Don't you want me for a
neighbor?"

"It isn't that," she lied. "I was just surprised that the
house was habitable already. It's been empty for
years."

Jordan grinned. "I put a little pressure on the
builder," he confessed.

Kendall wondered suddenly why he was in such a

hurry to establish residence. Was it true, what Dennis had said? Jordan Craig obviously was a man who knew what he wanted—and how to get those things done quickly. Once he had finished the house, would he begin to look past his own property toward hers? Cursing Dennis for planting doubts in her mind, an uneasy Kendall watched Jordan's car disappear down the drive.

Jordan had arrived back at his new home before the idea occurred to him. The construction crews he had hired to make the house habitable had gone for the night, and it was a relief not to hear the hammering and sawing that had gone on nonstop for days. But as he wandered through the newly framed section that had been burned out before, only one part of his thoughts was occupied with the quick progress the builder had made. He was thinking instead about Kendall and how hard she was working to make a go of it on her own. He had been like that once, struggling to make ends meet in a small machine shop. He still remembered how discouraging it had been to put all his energies into a business and still have to fight just to break even. He didn't have to worry about that anymore, but he hadn't forgotten that time of seemingly endless toil for so little reward.

Kendall was in that same position now. He had seen it today in things he hadn't noticed on his first visit, and as he noted the condition of the place, he had been tempted to offer his help. Then he'd realized that that would be the worst mistake he could make with her— just as it would have been for him in those early days of struggle. Kendall was proud; she wouldn't take a handout from anyone. In fact, he thought wryly, she would only have scorn for someone so foolish as to offer. She might desperately need help, but he knew that she would never ask for it. He admired that, but it was frustrating all the same, especially when he had so much to give.

So there had to be another way, some ruse he could use to offer her financial help without her being aware of it. An anonymous gift? He considered that for only an instant before rejecting the idea. Knowing Kendall, she'd probably be incensed at the thought that someone had been aware enough of her plight to send her a check. Undoubtedly she'd regard it as charity and never touch it. No, he had to be more clever than that.

Sighing, Jordan let himself into the main part of the house, opening the sliding glass doors in the living room to clear out the smell of fresh paint and new carpet. The contractor had been at work here, too. The kitchen gleamed with recently installed fixtures and tile counters; the living room furniture had been delivered and arranged by the decorator he had hired. Deep in thought, he went out onto the deck, pleased to see that the old, dilapidated barn had been razed and that the first of the several new ones he had planned was already under construction. The place was starting to take shape; in a week or two he would probably be able to move his horses in.

He frowned at that, realizing that that gave him even less time to think of a way to help Kendall. Once his own barn was ready, what excuse could he give for insisting that she keep his horses in hers?

No, he had to think of something else—something that would sound logical, something that would . . . Suddenly he had it. He considered the idea, examining it for flaws. There weren't any that he could see; it was perfect. Smiling to himself, Jordan went back inside. He had arrangements to make, details to work out. When he approached Kendall with this, the setting had to be absolutely right.

As he refined his plan later that night, Jordan refused to ask himself the real reason why he was so anxious to help Kendall Voss. He told himself that it was simply because he had the means, and that there was certainly no ulterior motive.

But even he knew, deep down, that that wasn't quite true.

Chapter 3

THE PHONE RANG JUST AS KENDALL WAS GULPING THE last of her breakfast coffee, and for a second or two she was tempted not to answer it. She had overslept, an unheard-of lapse for her, and the horses were waiting impatiently for their morning feed. She just couldn't seem to get going this morning; even after a shower, she still felt groggy and tired. She hadn't slept well last night, and what little sleep she'd managed had been filled with restless dreams, only fragments of which she could remember now. But the dreams had left her with a vague feeling of disquiet, and she didn't know why.

The phone rang again, and Kendall sighed. She had to answer it; it might be a new client. If it was, she couldn't afford to ignore it. Even with Jordan's horses here now, she still needed every penny she could get to pay the hay bill this month.

But when she answered, the caller wasn't a new client; it was Jordan Craig. As soon as she heard his voice, her pulse quickened, and she frowned. Trying to keep her voice under control, she managed to exchange the usual meaningless greetings without betraying her sudden breathlessness.

As always, Jordan got right to the point. "The reason I called is to invite you to dinner," he said.

Kendall felt herself gripping the phone even more tightly. "Dinner?" she echoed blankly.

"I know it's short notice, but I thought perhaps . . . tonight?"

"Tonight?" she heard herself say, and tried fiercely to get a grip on herself. She sounded like a parrot, she thought, and made another effort. "I'm sorry, but—"

"This will be a business dinner," Jordan said quickly, forestalling her refusal.

"A business dinner?" Kendall said, and closed her eyes, despising herself. What was wrong with her? She sounded like a complete idiot!

"Yes. I have a business proposition for you."

"What kind of a business proposition?" Kendall asked, forgetting her confusion in the rise of a sudden, ugly suspicion. Was this about buying her land? Because if it was . . .

"That's what I'd like to talk to you about over dinner," Jordan said. "Will you come?"

She had to play it cool, she thought. Nothing in the world would induce her to sell the ranch; she didn't care what kind of an offer he made. He could mention a sum that was ten times—a hundred times—what the property was worth, and she'd laugh in his face. But maybe she should go and hear what he had to say, she thought. Forewarned was forearmed, as her father used to say, and if Jordan told her that he wanted to buy her out, at least she'd know where he stood.

"You need a night away from that place," Jordan went on persuasively when she didn't answer. "And besides, I'm a good cook. Really, I am."

Despite herself, she had to smile at that. So he was going to cook dinner for her, was he? That was a switch. She was on the point of accepting after all when she realized with dismay that his invitation meant she would have to go to his home. Seeing him here, on her own ground, was difficult enough. How would it be when she was alone with him at his place? Even though she didn't trust him, she still couldn't deny the attraction she felt, and she hesitated again. Then she laughed at herself. If she was concerned about his making a pass at her, she really had nothing to worry about, did she? Jordan had never been anything but the perfect gentleman when he was here; he had never betrayed by a word or a glance that he intended to be anything else. So if he could be businesslike, she could be too. She had dealt with more clients than she could count, and she would just think of Jordan Craig as another in a long line. It was as simple as that.

"Kendall?"

"Yes, I'm here."

"About eight, then?"

She took a deep breath, wondering if she wouldn't be making a mistake after all. How could she treat Jordan as simply another client when she knew very well that that was the last thing in the world she wanted him to be? She wanted more than a business relationship with him, despite what he might be planning, and she might as well admit it. To herself, not to him, of course. Never to him.

"Eight is fine," she heard herself say.

"I'll pick you up—"

"No, no, that's not necessary," she said quickly. For some reason she couldn't explain, she would feel . . . safer . . . if she had her own car.

"All right," he said agreeably. "I'll see you at eight, then."

Kendall replaced the receiver slowly. A business proposition, she thought. Did that really mean what she thought it did? Well, if so, she would be prepared. There wasn't any use worrying about it, anyway. She had hours to wait until eight o'clock tonight, and in the meantime there were chores to do.

But by seven-thirty that night, Kendall was even more doubtful about this dinner Jordan had planned. Staring glumly at the contents of her closet, she wondered why she had ever agreed to go. Despite herself, she had existed in a state of anticipation all day, trying to convince herself that she was only interested in hearing what he had to say. But now that the hour was at hand, she felt a little like Cinderella on the night of the ball. What did one wear to a business dinner with a handsome, attractive man? Then she was disgusted with herself. If it was simply business he intended to discuss, what did it matter what she wore?

Frowning, she hauled out a navy pantsuit she always wore with a white blouse. It was very conservative, very correct . . . and awful. Grimacing, she put it back in the closet, choosing next a black wool dress with a high neckline and long sleeves, and staring at it critically. That wasn't right either, she thought; she'd look like a nun. She put that back as well and sat gloomily on the bed. She hadn't realized that her wardrobe was in such a sorry state; she hadn't given a thought to wearing anything but jeans and blouses for months. But she couldn't very well show up tonight in work clothes, so she'd have to chose something, and there was only one thing left—a dress that Tony had bought for her, one she'd never worn.

When she took it out from the back of the closet, it was still encased in the plastic bag the store had wrapped around it. As Kendall laid it on the bed, memories of the night Tony gave it to her flooded her mind. He had brought it home, presenting it with a flourish, obviously pleased with himself and wanting her to share in the sale of a horse he had just completed for a man back east. She found out the next day just what that sale had involved, and it was that night when they had their final fight. She had hidden the dress away, unable to bear the sight of it, and now when she saw the still-attached tags, she wanted to put it back again. Then she reconsidered. She had paid for this dress, she told herself grimly; she had paid dearly for it. Maybe by wearing it tonight she would be able to banish the ghosts that still lingered in her mind. Almost defiantly, she put it on.

Tony's taste in clothes had been much more flamboyant than hers, but as she inspected herself in the mirror, she had to admit that he had been right about this dress. Simply styled, with a rounded neckline and tulip sleeves, the persimmon silk was a good color for her. Her eyes suddenly looked a deeper green, and the tan she had gotten from working outdoors became more golden than brown. Satisfied, Kendall dabbed a little rarely used perfume behind her ears, took one last look at herself and went downstairs before she could change her mind and decide not to go.

Fortunately, the drive over took only a few minutes,

not long enough for her to become completely unnerved. Then, as she approached the turnoff, she
forgot her apprehension entirely in the sight that
greeted her. For as long as she could remember, the
gates that fronted the drive had been askew, half falling
off the hinges, spotted with rust. Now they had been
repaired and replaced, and new wood fences enclosed
the entire property. As Kendall drove through, she
noticed too that the driveway had been newly as-
phalted, and she thought wryly that Jordan had been
busy indeed.

Just how busy she saw a few moments later as she
continued on to the house. All the lights were ablaze,
and the new construction was clearly evident in the
glow of floodlights mounted under the eaves of the
freshly shingled roof. Amazed at the amount of work
that had been done in such a short time, Kendall
stopped the truck by the front door. Climbing out, she
glanced curiously around, thinking that Jordan must
have hired an army of builders. And gardeners, too,
she decided, noting the abundant plantings and the soft
sheen of new grass under the lights.

There were three wide flagstone steps to the front
door, but before she could try the bell, Jordan opened
the door, a greeting on his lips. He never finished the
sentence; instead, he just stood there a moment,
staring at her.

"This is the right night, isn't it?" Kendall asked
finally, pleased at the frank admiration in his eyes. She
was glad now that she had decided to wear the dress; it
was worth any number of bad memories just to see that
look on his face.

He started. "Yes. Yes, of course. Please—come in."

Delighted at the idea that he was the one at a loss for

words for a change, Kendall stepped past him into a flagstone foyer. As she turned to speak to him, she glimpsed something out of the corner of her eye and stopped, startled. When she saw what it was, she said, "I didn't know you had a cat!"

Jordan frowned. "I don't."

She pointed at the huge black and white tom, who was surveying them disdainfully from his position behind a giant potted fern in the entry. "Tell him that," she said.

"How did he get in again?" Jordan asked, exasperated. "He seems to . . . to *materialize* whenever I'm not looking." He made a threatening gesture in the cat's direction, but the big tom just looked at him and yawned, obviously not in the least impressed.

Trying not to smile, Kendall commented, "He looks a little . . . disheveled, doesn't he?" She didn't know which to be more amused at: Jordan's resigned expression, or the cat itself. It easily weighed twenty pounds, and seemed accustomed to defending itself—poorly, Kendall thought, for half of one ear was missing, and an old battle scar over one eye gave it a squint.

"Ugly thing," Jordan muttered.

"Oh, I don't know. I think he's got character." She bent down, calling to the animal. It came at once, rubbing against her leg and rumbling a satisfied purr. It glanced up at Jordan then with what could only be described as a satisfied smirk, and Kendall laughed aloud. When she straightened, she looked at Jordan with amusement. "I think you've got yourself a cat," she said.

"Why don't you take him home? He seems to like you better than me. The only thing he does when I'm around is growl!"

"No, thanks. I've got too many as it is."

Sighing, Jordan bent down, intending to grab the animal and put it out the front door. It slipped from his grasp with practiced ease, disappearing into the hall to the right with a flick of its tail. Jordan uttered a disgusted sound, and Kendall tried not to laugh again as they went into the living room.

"Would you like a drink?" Jordan asked, warning her with a look that he'd had enough discussion about the cat.

"Oh . . . a glass of wine, if you have it."

She watched him as he went to the bar at the side of the room, and she realized with surprise that she wasn't nervous anymore. The cat had broken the ice between them, and when Jordan returned with her glass, she was able to smile naturally and say, "You've done wonders with this place already. I'm impressed."

"It's starting to take shape. But unfortunately, we haven't had time to do much with the new barn."

"I don't know why not," Kendall teased. "It seems such a simple thing—building a place from the ground up. And after all, you've had almost a whole week already!"

"Would you like to see the plans for the barn?" Jordan asked, laughing with her. "I . . . er . . . have to see to something in the kitchen."

Kendall had been aware of tantalizing odors from that direction since she came in. Curious to see if he really was preparing the meal, she said, "Would you like some help?"

"No, you just sit there and relax. Here, these are the blueprints. Why don't you glance at them so you can tell me what you think while we're having dinner?"

Kendall wasn't just surprised when she unrolled the

blueprints; she was amazed. Jordan didn't plan on a single barn; she counted three, plus various pasture shelters, a covered riding ring, and a round, roofed pen. As she gazed at the notations for wash racks, tack rooms, foaling stalls with video cameras, and an office with adjoining bath and shower in the main barn, she couldn't help feeling a small stab of jealousy. As much as she loved her own ranch, she had once had dreams of a place like this, but she knew it was impossible—right now, anyway. But as she studied the plans, she had no doubt that Jordan would accomplish it all, and more.

Fragments of her conversation with Dennis Atchison intruded into her thoughts just then, and the envy was replaced with a definite feeling of unease. Was Dennis right? Jordan had forty acres, and, judging from these plans, he was planning on utilizing every one of them. Would it be enough for him—or, as Dennis had so slyly suggested, would Jordan want more?

She thought of the way he had glanced around when he was at the ranch the other day, and her uneasiness increased. Had he been assessing her property with the idea of annexing it to his own? The idea wasn't so farfetched now that she saw what he intended to do here, and she became even more convinced that the purpose of this business dinner was to sound her out about selling. Well, she had her answer prepared, she thought grimly, and nothing was going to change her mind, no matter how difficult it might be to stand firm. She had been in the horse business too long not to know what happened to smaller ranches when wealthy investors moved in. Several of the people she had known over the years, in fact, had surrendered to the pressure of big money, simply because they just couldn't compete. They had been forced eventually to sell out and move somewhere else—or get out of horses completely. It had happened to one of her father's closest friends when Kaylene Van Zandt decided to build her ranch. Kaylene had been like a bulldozer, gobbling up all the property around her until her place was the biggest around. Did Jordan intend to do the same thing? He could try, Kendall thought defiantly, but he wasn't going to do that to her.

"Well, what do you think?"

Kendall started at the sound of his voice, trying to keep her expression carefully neutral when she looked up at him. "It certainly looks like it's going to be a big enterprise," she said.

Jordan smiled, taking the plans from her and tossing them nonchalantly on the coffee table. The gesture wasn't lost on Kendall; he was obviously playing this casually, trying to disarm her. Unfortunately for him, it wasn't going to work.

"We can talk about it over dinner, if you like," he said, offering her his hand to help her up from the couch.

Despite her resolve, Kendall found herself nodding in agreement. He didn't release her hand when she stood, and the pressure of his fingers evoked some almost-forgotten feeling in her. Reminding herself that he might be one of those greedy investors she despised didn't do any good; at that moment, with her hand in his, he was just a man, one she was still foolishly attracted to.

"Did I tell you how beautiful you look tonight?" Jordan asked, gazing at her with admiration. "That color becomes you."

Kendall could hardly answer. When he looked at her like that, she felt breathless, poised on the edge of an emotion she didn't want to acknowledge. "Thank you," she managed finally, thinking that he looked even more handsome tonight that he had before. The diffused living room light made his dark hair gleam and softened the lean lines of his face. He was wearing a cream-colored shirt under a beige sweater that had to be cashmere, and he looked casual and sophisticated at the same time. Like an advertisement in a magazine, she thought confusedly, one of those impossibly attractive men who you knew always said the right things.

But Jordan wasn't the pretty-boy type of model; his features were a little too rugged for that, his expression and the way he moved much more . . . masculine. She could imagine him chairing important conferences with authority—or rafting down a white-water river with equal ease.

It seemed that he was also adept in the kitchen. Jordan laughed when he saw her expression as they went into the dining room, but he was obviously pleased, too. "I hope you like rack of lamb," he said, seating her at the table. "It's about the only thing I can cook—except for bacon and eggs."

Kendall doubted that. From what little she knew of Jordan Craig, she shouldn't be surprised at any accomplishment of his, including the meal, which was superb. When she mentioned it, and how nice it was to be pampered like this, Jordan said, "You should pamper yourself more often. Take a day off once in a while."

Oh, if only she could! Kendall thought. She couldn't remember the last time she'd had a whole day—or even part of one—all to herself. She thought longingly of the stack of novels that remained unread by her bed because she was too tired at night to do more than glance over horse journals; she thought of the bottle of bubble bath, still unopened after her birthday last year because there was never time for more than a quick shower.

"You don't look like a man who takes much time off either," she said, trying not to think of such luxuries as reading, or soaking in a hot tub.

Something flickered across his face, a look of pain—or regret—that was gone in an instant. "I've had to learn to take time off this past year," he said, his voice suddenly flat.

Kendall wasn't sure what to say to that. Some instinct warned her not to pursue the subject, so she said lightly, "I imagine that you won't have much time off once you start construction on the barns."

"Oh, that's already begun," he said, trying to match her mood. "We should have the first one done in a couple of weeks."

"So soon?"

He smiled. "As you can see, I have a builder who works as hard as you do."

"What does Mrs. Craig have to say about all this?" Kendall asked, and then was appalled. She hadn't meant to say anything about a wife; she could have bitten her tongue.

"There is no Mrs. Craig," Jordan said.

His voice was so harsh that Kendall actually flinched. "I'm sorry," she stammered. "I didn't . . ."

Jordan saw her expression and looked contrite. "No, I'm the one who should apologize," he said, his voice low and still colored with some inner pain. "I didn't mean to sound so . . ." He stopped and tried again. "My wife died last year," he said finally. "It was . . . an accident."

Kendall gazed at him. "I know how you feel," she said quietly.

"Do you?"

Wincing at the hard challenge in his voice, she answered, "Yes. I lost my husband last year. It was an accident, too."

This time it was Jordan who cringed. "I'm sorry. I didn't know."

"There's no reason why you should have," Kendall said simply. "It's . . . it's not something I like to talk about."

She couldn't help it; images of the night Tony died flashed into her mind just then: the terrifying knock on the door at two a.m.; the sight of the policeman standing on the doorstep; the quiet request for her to accompany him.

"Are you all right?"

Kendall closed her eyes briefly. "Yes," she said, and wondered if she ever really would be. She summoned a shaky smile. "I keep telling myself it's all in the past, but—"

"But it never is, is it?"

She shook her head, and their eyes met in shared understanding. Seeing the compassion in his glance, she once again had the absurd desire to throw herself into his arms. It had been so long since she'd been held by a man, she thought longingly. Sometimes in the middle of the night she would awaken, clutching the pillow, wishing she had someone to comfort her, just to hold her until she slept again. She missed that even more than she missed a man's physical strength around the ranch. She could do it all—the fence mending and the stall cleaning and all the thousand and one chores that were required—if she just had someone to hold her at night.

Then she hardened her heart. She'd had a man to hold her once, she reminded herself, and it hadn't been worth it. It seemed to her now that love and pain were inseparably entwined, and she couldn't go through all that hurt again, not for any man. She had trusted Tony with her love, and he had betrayed her in the worst possible way. She didn't think she could ever trust a man again.

"No," she said. "It never is in the past."

"Kendall—"

"Please. I don't want to talk about it anymore. I—"

Just then, startling them both, the cat jumped on the table. Before either of them could move, the big tom had spied the remains of the lamb and pounced on it. Snatching the bone from the platter, the cat jumped off the table. He disappeared in the direction of the kitchen, triumphantly carrying his prize. The whole thing happened so fast that neither Jordan nor Kendall could move; they stared after him in astonishment, unsure whether they had really witnessed the theft or not. Then Kendall saw Jordan's face and burst into laughter. He looked so outraged that it was absolutely comical.

"I'll break his scrawny neck!" Jordan shouted, leaping up from his chair. "He'll never do a thing like that again—not if I have anything to say about it!"

Kendall couldn't stop laughing. "You'll never catch him," she sputtered between bouts of laughter. "He's probably miles away by now, enjoying a gourmet meal!"

Jordan glared at her. "That wasn't funny!"

Covering her mouth with her hand, Kendall sput-

uired—if she just had someone to hold her

ardened her heart. She'd had a man to
, she reminded herself, and it hadn't been
emed to her now that love and pain were
ntwined, and she couldn't go through all
n, not for any man. She had trusted Tony
, and he had betrayed her in the worst
She didn't think she could ever trust a

said. "It never is in the past."
"

on't want to talk about it anymore. I—"
artling them both, the cat jumped on the
either of them could move, the big tom
remains of the lamb and pounced on it.
bone from the platter, the cat jumped off
disappeared in the direction of the
phantly carrying his prize. The whole
d so fast that neither Jordan nor Kendall
hey stared after him in astonishment,
r they had really witnessed the theft or
ndall saw Jordan's face and burst into
oked so outraged that it was absolutely

s scrawny neck!" Jordan shouted, leap-
chair. "He'll never do a thing like that
have anything to say about it!"
dn't stop laughing. "You'll never catch
ered between bouts of laughter. "He's
away by now, enjoying a gourmet

at her. "That wasn't funny!"
mouth with her hand, Kendall sput-

emotion she didn't want to acknowledge. "Thank you," she managed finally, thinking that he looked even more handsome tonight that he had before. The diffused living room light made his dark hair gleam and softened the lean lines of his face. He was wearing a cream-colored shirt under a beige sweater that had to be cashmere, and he looked casual and sophisticated at the same time. Like an advertisement in a magazine, she thought confusedly, one of those impossibly attractive men who you knew always said the right things.

But Jordan wasn't the pretty-boy type of model; his features were a little too rugged for that, his expression and the way he moved much more . . . masculine. She could imagine him chairing important conferences with authority—or rafting down a white-water river with equal ease.

It seemed that he was also adept in the kitchen. Jordan laughed when he saw her expression as they went into the dining room, but he was obviously pleased, too. "I hope you like rack of lamb," he said, seating her at the table. "It's about the only thing I can cook—except for bacon and eggs."

Kendall doubted that. From what little she knew of Jordan Craig, she shouldn't be surprised at any accomplishment of his, including the meal, which was superb. When she mentioned it, and how nice it was to be pampered like this, Jordan said, "You should pamper yourself more often. Take a day off once in a while."

Oh, if only she could! Kendall thought. She couldn't remember the last time she'd had a whole day—or even part of one—all to herself. She thought longingly of the stack of novels that remained unread by her bed because she was too tired at night to do more than glance over horse journals; she thought of the bottle of bubble bath, still unopened after her birthday last year because there was never time for more than a quick shower.

"You don't look like a man who takes much time off either," she said, trying not to think of such luxuries as reading, or soaking in a hot tub.

Something flickered across his face, a look of pain—or regret—that was gone in an instant. "I've had to learn to take time off this past year," he said, his voice suddenly flat.

Kendall wasn't sure what to say to that. Some instinct warned her not to pursue the subject, so she said lightly, "I imagine that you won't have much time off once you start construction on the barns."

"Oh, that's already begun," he said, trying to match her mood. "We should have the first one done in a couple of weeks."

"So soon?"

He smiled. "As you can see, I have a builder who works as hard as you do."

"What does Mrs. Craig have to say about all this?" Kendall asked, and then was appalled. She hadn't meant to say anything about a wife; she could have bitten her tongue.

"There is no Mrs. Craig," Jordan said.

His voice was so harsh that Kendall actually flinched. "I'm sorry," she stammered. "I didn't . . ."

Jordan saw her expression and looked contrite. "No, I'm the one who should apologize," he said, his voice low and still colored with some inner pain. "I didn't mean to sound so . . ." He stopped and tried again. "My wife died last year," he said finally. "It was . . . an accident."

Kendall gazed at hi
said quietly.

"Do you?"

Wincing at the ha
answered, "Yes. I lost
accident, too."

This time it was Jor
didn't know."

"There's no reason
said simply. "It's . . . i
about."

She couldn't help it;
flashed into her mind ju
the door at two a.m.
standing on the doorste
accompany him.

"Are you all right?"

Kendall closed her e
wondered if she ever re
shaky smile. "I keep t
but—"

"But it never is, is i

She shook her head
understanding. Seeing
she once again had th
into his arms. It had b
by a man, she thoug
middle of the night s
pillow, wishing she ha
hold her until she sl
more than she missed
the ranch. She could
the stall cleaning and

that were re
at night.

Then she
hold her on
worth it. It
inseparably
that hurt ag
with her lo
possible wa
man again.

"No," sh
"Kendall-
"Please.
Just then,
table. Befor
had spied t
Snatching tl
the table.
kitchen, tri
thing happe
could move
unsure whe
not. Then
laughter. H
comical.

"I'll breal
ing up from
again—not i

Kendall c
him," she s
probably m
meal!"

Jordan gla
Covering

tered again, "No, it wasn't," and started laughing harder than ever.

Jordan stared at her, still outraged. Then, reluctantly, he smiled. An instant later he was laughing uproariously too. "At least he has good taste," he said. "Maybe I'll keep him after all."

"I don't think you have a choice," Kendall said, wiping her eyes. "After a dinner like that, you're never going to get rid of him. And that reminds me—where *did* you learn to cook like this? You'd put a lot of women to shame, including me."

A fleeting expression of sadness crossed Jordan's face, but he answered with determined lightness. "It was self-preservation, I guess. I got tired of eating out all the time, and after a while peanut butter sandwiches lose their appeal."

Kendall agreed wholeheartedly with that. She'd slapped together quite a few of those herself this past year, simply because she was too tired at night to make anything else.

"Well, now that the cat has cleared the table," Jordan said, "why don't we have coffee in the living room? Unless you'd prefer a brandy?"

Kendall shook her head. She'd already had too much of the wine he had served with the meal; brandy would probably push her over the edge. "Coffee is fine," she said, and followed him into the kitchen to help carry things in.

He handed her cups and saucers, and as he did so, their hands touched. Once again Kendall felt that tingling thrill of contact, and when their eyes met she was elated to see that he felt it too. For a breathless instant they just stared at each other, and the thought flashed into her mind that he was going to kiss her. Did she want him to? Quite suddenly, she knew that she did. She had wanted him to kiss her from that first day. So she waited now, heart thumping madly, hardly able to endure the anticipation she felt. She was actually turning to put the cups back on the counter when he spoke.

"Why don't you take those into the living room? I'll be right there with the coffee."

Kendall felt like a complete fool. Had she imagined that look in his eyes? She must have. He obviously hadn't felt the same thrill she had when they touched; he hadn't felt anything at all if the only thing on his mind was the blasted coffee. Turning away before he could see the painful flush staining her cheeks, Kendall fled to the living room. Her hands were shaking so badly from embarrassment and anger that the cups rattled on their saucers, and it was only by a fierce effort that she managed to set them down gently on the coffee table and not fling them in fury against the wall.

Hands clenched, she tried to get hold of herself. She had to be in control before he came in; she didn't want him to know how foolish she felt, and she certainly didn't want him to apologize for that awkward moment in the kitchen. An apology would be even worse than not acknowledging it at all.

Pressing her palms against her hot cheeks, she closed her eyes. Oh, it was crystal clear to her now that Jordan Craig had no interest in her as a woman. She should have realized that before she made an idiot of herself.

But she *had* realized it, she told herself fiercely; she just hadn't wanted to accept it. She had been attracted to him from the start, and she had concocted this absurd fantasy about him because he had invited her to dinner tonight. She hadn't wanted to believe that this was planned for some business purpose of his; until a few minutes ago she had cherished the hope that he had . . . something else in mind. Obviously, she'd been wrong.

All right, then, she told herself angrily, if that's what he wants, that's what he'll get. She could be all business too.

On that thought, she seated herself resolutely in one of the chairs flanking the couch. When Jordan came in with the carafe, she was able to look coolly at him and thank him for the meal. Then she said, "You told me you had a business proposition."

He seemed a little taken aback by her abrupt change in manner, and for a second or two he didn't answer. Kendall reached forward and calmly poured herself a cup of coffee, enjoying his discomfiture. I can play your little game too, Mr. Craig, she thought, gazing at him over the rim of her cup. From now on, things between us are going to be strictly professional, no matter how I feel.

Felt, she amended. Whatever romantic ideas she had entertained about him were under control now. Especially, she thought grimly, if he was going to make an offer for her ranch.

Jordan sat down on the couch and poured himself a cup too. "All right," he said. "I'd like to hire you as my agent."

Kendall stared at him, her indifferent pose forgotten. "Your agent!" she said. "But that's . . . that's ridiculous!"

Leaving his cup untouched, Jordan took a cigarette from the container on the table. Lighting it with a matching gold lighter, he sat back, studying her. "Why?" he asked simply.

His even gaze unnerved her. Casting around frantically for a logical reason to refuse, she said, "But you already have a bloodstock agent—you told me so yourself."

He shook his head. "I said that someone gave me advice."

"Well, whoever it was, they knew what they were doing. You certainly don't need me."

"Yes, I do. You've seen the plans I have for this place. I'm not going to all that trouble to populate those barns with inferior stock."

"You don't *have* inferior stock! I'd match those mares of yours with any in the country!"

He made a dismissive gesture. "That was a fluke. No, I need someone to help me formulate a breeding program, and then help me implement it. I think you would do an excellent job."

"Why?" she asked flatly.

"Because you know horses, especially Arabians. And I—" He hesitated a fraction. "I don't."

Kendall knew how much the admission cost him, and for a second or two she wavered. Then she looked at him again and knew that she had to refuse. She was far too attracted to him, even now, despite her vows to herself. If she worked so closely with him, she wouldn't be able to maintain any emotional distance at all. It just wouldn't work; she knew it wouldn't. She would never be able to hide her feelings for him if she saw him so frequently. It would be impossible to pretend that theirs was just a client/agent relationship—especially when she knew she would want so much more.

"I'm sorry," she began.

"It will be worth your time," he said. "I'll double the usual commission."

She stared at him again, this time in outrage. Did he honestly think that *money* was at the root of her refusal? How blind could the man be?

"It isn't that!" she blurted thoughtlessly.

"What, then?"

She stopped herself in the nick of time, aghast at the thought of confessing the real reason. Unable suddenly to sit still, she sprang up from the chair and walked to the sliding glass doors at the end of the living room. Vaguely she noticed the excavation outside, intended to be a pool, but she really didn't see it. She took a deep breath, and then turned around again.

He was right behind her, so close that she almost bumped into him. She jumped back.

"I didn't mean to offend you," he said quietly.

"You didn't offend me," she replied angrily. "It's just—" Suddenly she found her excuse, and she seized on it like a lifeline. "It's just that I don't have time to—"

"I'm not going to fill this place with horses right away," he pointed out reasonably. "I don't even have the barns built yet."

She was too aware of him standing so close to her. When he was so near, she couldn't think straight. She couldn't think at all. Sidling past him, she went back to the coffee table and poured another cup of coffee she didn't even want.

"I'm sorry, Jordan, but I—"

"Can't we at least give it a try?" he asked. "I want to get those mares in foal, and from what everybody says, I should make arrangements soon or the season will be over. I had hoped that you would be able to recommend a suitable stallion—for a finder's fee, of course."

"I *told* you, it isn't the money!"

But this time her protest wasn't quite so vehement. Already her breeder's mind had begun running over possibilities, and she had to admit that matching those mares of his to suitable stallions would be exciting. Especially, she thought enviously, when outrageous stud fees weren't a consideration.

Jordan sensed her weakening. "I'd really appreciate your help on this," he said, coming over to stand beside her. "And if you find that just choosing a stallion is too time-consuming for you, I won't ask anymore. Is that fair?"

She didn't know whether it was fair or not. When he looked at her that way, she seemed to lose all will to resist him. Furious with herself for being such a weakling, she said, "All right. We'll try it. But if it doesn't work out—"

"I know; I know. We'll just take it one step at a time," he said, grinning at her. "I think this calls for champagne, don't you?"

Before she could object, he had brought out a bottle and two glasses. After pouring for them, he ticked the rim of her glass with his, saying, "To a profitable partnership—on both sides!"

Kendall drank slowly, watching him and wondering dismally what had happened to all her resolve. Not two minutes ago she had vowed to refuse whatever he asked. Now she was involved in this insane partnership with him.

And that's exactly what it was, she thought glumly: insane. She couldn't trust herself with him; she knew she couldn't. There would come a time when, no matter how hard she tried not to, she would betray herself with a word or a look.

"I—," Jordan said, and stopped, his voice suddenly husky.

She didn't move when he took her glass from her hand and put both glasses on the coffee table. She didn't move when he put his arms around her. She couldn't; her legs were so weak that she thought for an instant she might fall. Then Jordan tipped her chin up with his hand.

"I've wanted to do this from the first moment I saw you . . . ," he said, and bent his head to kiss her.

At the first touch Kendall closed her eyes, giving herself up to the sensation she had anticipated for so long. His lips were warm and smooth, gently demanding at first, then moving with increasing pressure. Kendall had no wish to resist him; she welcomed the tightening of his arms around her, the feel of his strong hands at her waist, pulling her closer to him. Raising her arms, she caressed the back of his neck, running her hands through his hair, luxuriating in the texture of it, drawing his head down even closer to hers.

They broke apart finally, gasping. Kendall fought the impulse to put a hand to her lips. They felt almost bruised with the intensity of her passionate response to him, and she was appalled by her uncontrollable reaction. She knew that if he had begun making love to her, she couldn't have—wouldn't have—refused him. Aghast at the thought, she knew she had to stop this now, before she lost all control.

"I think I'd better go," she said shakily.

Jordan seemed a little shaken himself. He didn't object, as she had half hoped he would; he nodded instead. "I'll walk you out to the car."

Outside, with the night air mercifully cooling her

face, Kendall said awkwardly, "Thank you for the dinner."

Jordan's eyes seemed very black. "My pleasure."

"Jordan . . . about what happened just now . . ."

"Yes?"

He wasn't going to make it any easier for her, was he? Angry at the thought, she said quickly, "I don't think it should happen again. I'll try acting as your agent for a while, but . . . but that's all our relationship is going to be. Is that agreed?"

He hesitated for only a moment, searching her eyes. Finally he said stiffly, "Yes. You're right. I think that would be best."

What else could she say after that? Feeling even more awkward, she got into her car. Driving away without looking back, she told herself that she was glad she had defined their relationship so firmly, and that he had agreed. He was obviously just as sorry as she was about the incident, and that was perfectly fine with her.

But her lips still burned from his kiss, and her body ached from unfulfilled need long after she went to bed that night. She woke the next morning feeling tired and out-of-sorts, and as she stumbled downstairs to make coffee, she wondered bitterly how well Jordan had slept. Probably like a rock, she thought, banging the kettle on top of the stove. As she waited for the water to boil, Kendall sat dismally at the table, wondering why she had agreed to act as his agent. It had to be all that wine, she thought, holding her aching head in her hands. She was never going to drink again.

Jordan hadn't slept well at all. At the same time that Kendall was banging around in her kitchen, he was sitting in his, staring moodily at the dregs of his third cup of coffee. The ashtray before him was littered with cigarette butts, and he glanced at it distastefully before pushing it away. Last night's dishes were still stacked on the counter, and the mess reflected his state of mind— and the disaster he had made of the evening.

He hadn't meant to kiss her, he thought; he had steeled himself against it the whole night, in fact. It was just that he'd been so surprised to see her in that dress. She had looked so different, he thought—softer, more feminine, even more desirable than she always did. Even in jeans and boots she could arouse him, and seeing her in that dress had completely thrown him off-balance.

Frowning, he got up and wandered over to the kitchen window. From his position he could see where the barns and paddocks were going to be, and he wondered what he had gotten himself into. This whole project had started as a form of therapy, and he hadn't thought he'd get so involved. It had been a way to pass the time until he was ready to resume control of the company again, but now he wondered if he really wanted to do that. He'd never thought of Los Angeles as a rat race before; he had enjoyed the challenge and the excitement, even the pressure. But now . . .

Now there was Kendall Voss, with her expressive green eyes and her refusal to knuckle under despite the odds. She had taught him a lot, and not only about horses. She was so different from Marie, who had been sweet and fluttery and . . . so dependent on him. He couldn't imagine Kendall being dependent on any man; it just wasn't in her nature. Maybe that's what intrigued him about her; she was so proud, so determined to make it on her own. Frowning again, he moved away from the window. The construction crews were due to arrive soon, and he wanted to talk over some changes with the builder.

Jordan was dressed and outside, watching the trucks coming up the drive, when he realized something that made him pause. This morning was the first time he had been able to think about Marie without feeling that crushing weight of guilt about her death. He had loved his wife; for ten years he had given her everything he could. He had told himself he was fortunate to have a wife who was so beautiful and gracious, who ran his home and their social engagements with ease. But he had wished so often that she had been interested in being more than just his wife; he had tried to encourage her to develop other interests. He had been suffocating under Marie's clinging dependence, and he had wondered for months if a trial separation wouldn't be best. He needed some breathing space, and Marie had to find out that she could manage without him. But every time he'd thought to broach the subject, he could picture the bewildered hurt in her eyes, and he couldn't do it. Her only crime, if that's what it was, had been loving him too much, and he had despised himself for not being able to return such blind devotion. Her love had imprisoned him, and in a horrible way, he had been almost relieved to be free of it.

And now there was Kendall. He had thought up the idea of having her act as his agent because he wanted to help her without being obvious. It seemed the perfect solution because they would both benefit. The only problem was that he was more attracted to her than he wanted to admit. The thought had crossed his mind more than once that what he really wanted was a personal relationship with her. He had been relieved when she insisted that it was going to be all business between them; it was all he could do to stop at that one kiss. But now he wondered how he was going to keep his distance despite their agreement.

Especially, he thought bleakly, if all he could think about was how she felt in his arms, and how much he wanted to make love to her.

Chapter 4

THE SCOTTSDALE SHOW AND SALE SEASON OPENED THE following week, and as the residents prepared for the influx of visitors from all parts of the country, even from around the world, Kendall pored over the sales brochures with an eagle eye.

This was a time when, in addition to the numerous open-house parties and tours, many of the big ranches organized their own auctions—some by invitation only. Potential buyers were required to establish lines of credit in advance, and Kendall knew from past experience that millions of dollars were involved. The prices of Arabian horses had zoomed astronomically in the past few years, and only those buyers who could establish elite financial status were invited to the more prestigious sales. Unfortunately for Kendall, the Van Zandt sale was one of them.

Even before she studied the brochure, she knew that

Kaylene Van Zandt would be offering some of the finest—and most expensive—horses. Trying hard to put aside her dislike of the woman, Kendall studied the Van Zandt sales list in particular and, after mulling it over for a few days, selected four possible candidates for Jordan. Any one of the horses she had decided on would be a valuable addition to Jordan's stable, and the day before the sale, she gathered her courage and went over to talk to him about it.

As she had promised, she had also chosen several stallion candidates for the mares he already owned, but as she drove the short distance to his place, she wondered why she hadn't just called him with the information. She tried to tell herself that it was easier to go over the list with him in person, but she knew that that was just an excuse, and a poor one at that. The truth, she thought, squirming, was that she wanted to see him again. She hadn't even talked to him since the night he had invited her for dinner, and as the days had passed since then, she hadn't been able to get him out of her mind.

She hadn't been able to get his kiss out of her mind, either—or her response to it. She knew she was playing with fire by deliberately going to see him again, but she couldn't help it. He was like some compulsion with her—fascinating and dangerous.

She had never met a man like him; that was part of the fascination. She couldn't figure him out at all. One minute he was charming and relaxed; the next he had withdrawn because she had unknowingly trod on some private mental ground. He reminded her of a kaleidoscope she had had as a child: constantly shifting colors and designs, never the same pattern twice. She didn't know anything about him, really; it was all rumors and conjecture. But even if only part of what she'd heard was true, she had no business seeing a man who might be planning to take her ranch away from her. A man who, she thought unwillingly, was still grieving over his wife.

She knew what guilt and grief could do; she had suffered the same tortures herself. It had taken her a long time to get over Tony, and even a year after his death she still had unexpected lapses into remorse. Having to work so hard and sacrifice so much to undo the damage he had done had helped; anger went a long way toward healing old wounds, and she'd been angry for a long time. But how would she feel if she had loved Tony unreservedly to the end, as Jordan had obviously loved his wife? Would the pain and the sense of loss remain, coloring every other emotion? Sighing, she thought they might.

The worst of it was that, even knowing all these things, she couldn't seem to help herself—or deny the anticipation she felt as she drove through the new gates and stopped the truck in front of Jordan's house.

There was no answer to the doorbell, so she followed the sounds of activity coming from behind the house. Rounding the corner, she stopped in surprise. The original, falling-down barn had been almost completely replaced; carpenters were working on the roof, while other workers were fencing individual paddocks. The place was a hive of activity, and in the center of it was Jordan, deep in conversation with another man. They both glanced up as she approached, Jordan warily, the other man with curiosity.

"You're up early," Jordan said cautiously as she walked up to them.

"I came over to talk to you about some sale horses," Kendall said, wishing more than ever that she had just decided to phone. Now that she'd said it aloud, her excuse sounded so transparent that she was sure he would guess the real reason she had come was simply because she wanted to see him. She didn't dare meet his eyes; she made herself glance casually around instead. "But I can see how busy you are, so maybe I'd better come back another time."

"No, no, that's all right," Jordan said quickly. He gestured, forcing a laugh. "You can see that everyone is getting along fine without my supervision. We were just going inside to have a cup of coffee, in fact, and leave them to it. Oh, Kendall, this is Martin Holbrook. As my so-called financial adviser, he's the one who's really responsible for all this. Martin, Kendall Voss."

They shook hands, Kendall forgetting some of her discomfort over Jordan in the genuine smile of this man with his interested blue eyes. "I'm pleased to meet you, Miss Voss," Martin said. "I've heard a lot about you from Jordan."

Kendall didn't want to pursue that; she could just imagine what he'd been told. Returning his smile, she asked, "Are you a horse owner too?"

"Heaven's no!" Martin answered with such an expression of horror that Kendall had to laugh. "I'm merely a spectator on this project, perfectly content to view from afar—and the farther the better!"

"Hardly that," Jordan commented dryly, "since you're here today. And don't forget, you were the one who talked me into getting involved with horses in the first place."

"It was just a suggestion, if you recall," Martin

countered with a wink in Kendall's direction. "I never dreamed you'd take me so seriously."

"Now you tell me!"

"Well, it can't be all bad if it lets you meet beautiful women like Miss Voss."

Kendall colored at the compliment, and on impulse said, "I think you should come around more often, Mr. Holbrook. Maybe your gallantry might rub off on someone else we know."

Martin seemed delighted at her thrust. "If you mean Jordan, I'm afraid it's too late for that. I've been trying to smooth those rough edges of his for years, all to no avail."

"I can see that," Kendall replied demurely, enjoying the look on Jordan's face.

"I'm going to the kitchen for some coffee," Jordan said, glaring at them both. "When you two finish my character assassination, maybe you'll join me."

Martin shook his head. "I'm afraid I don't have time. I've got a flight to catch, and I just might make it to the airport if I leave now. It was nice meeting you, Miss Voss. I hope we see each other again."

"I hope so too," Kendall said sincerely. "But it's a shame you can't stay on for a few days. The show season is just starting here, and some of the sales are really spectacular."

"Yes," Jordan said, straight-faced. "You never know, Martin—if you stayed awhile, you might just get caught up in the excitement and buy a horse yourself."

"That's why I'm taking the first plane out," Martin said with a shudder. "You can call me with the next bit of devastating financial news when I'm safely back in the office. "I wouldn't be surprised if, when I visit again, you have a whole flock of horses here."

"Herd, Martin. The word is herd."

"Whatever. All eating their heads off, I'm sure, and clamoring for more."

Kendall laughed, thinking that he wasn't far wrong. But as they watched him walk to his car before they went inside, she started to feel nervous with Jordan again, and she blurted, "He doesn't look like a financial adviser."

Jordan was amused. "What's a financial adviser supposed to look like?" he asked as they entered the kitchen.

Kendall accepted a cup of coffee from him, telling herself that she had to calm down. She was here on business; it was nothing more than that. "Oh, someone who's solemn and sober all the time. Serious, with all those figures on his mind, I guess."

Jordan sat at the table with her. His eyes twinkling, he said, "I suspect that Martin does have figures on his mind all the time—but not the kind you mean."

He laughed at the look on her face. "I'm sorry. That makes him sound like a playboy—which he's not. Although he does happen to be eligible. Since his divorce, he's had half the women in Los Angeles trying to snare him, but he keeps slipping loose. He likes the attention, but knowing Marty, he has no intention of getting married or involved again—not for a long time, anyway."

And what about you? Kendall wondered. Are you pursued by the other half of the women? Do you enjoy the attention too?

"I can see why," she said lightly. "He's an attractive man."

Jordan raised an eyebrow at that, obviously tempted

to pursue the subject. Instead he said, "You mentioned something about a list of horses . . ."

As Kendall pulled the paper from her pocket, she wondered why she always felt this tension between them. It was unnerving, never knowing when she might say the wrong thing—or when he might take offense at something she hadn't said at all. Sighing inwardly with frustration, she put the list in front of him.

But as she started going over the bloodlines of the horses she had written down, she was aware of Jordan's eyes on her instead of on the paper. Once or twice, as she was giving her reasons for selecting these particular animals, she glanced up at him and was unnerved again by his silent scrutiny. She sat back when she had finished, wishing he would say something. Anything at all, she thought irritably, would be helpful at this point.

"You put a lot of thought into this, didn't you?" he asked at last, gazing at her with that strange expression she couldn't fathom. "Why?"

She wanted to ask why he was staring at her, why he had been staring at her the whole time she was trying to explain things to him. But she couldn't ask, and so, because she was annoyed with herself and with him, she answered flippantly, "That's what you're paying me for, isn't it?"

As soon as the words were out of her mouth, she regretted them. Now she had no doubt what he was thinking; he told her—not so much in the words themselves, but in the tone in which he said them. "Yes. I guess it is," he agreed coolly. "I appreciate all the trouble you've taken."

"Well," she said weakly, "I hope you find something there you like. If not, there are other sales."

"But none as prestigious as the Van Zandt sale, right?"

She stared at him. Was prestige all he cared about? She was tempted to tell him that she hadn't chosen these horses because of their prestige, but because of their bloodlines. If he'd been paying attention to her, he would have realized that. Buying a horse from Kaylene was no great honor, she thought irately; in fact, she would have preferred it if these animals were being offered by anyone but that woman. He was just lucky that she'd been able to put aside her distaste for Kaylene long enough to go through that list. If she had allowed her dislike to affect her judgment, she wouldn't have given the Van Zandt horses a second glance.

But she wasn't going to get into an argument with him about Kaylene; the woman wasn't worth that much of her time. Nor, after a remark like that, was Jordan Craig, she decided angrily. Seething, she stood and said, "No. None as prestigious as this, if that's what you're worried about. Good-bye, Mr. Craig. Good luck at the sale."

He stood with her. "You're not going?"

She looked at him, surprised at the question. "Why should I go?"

"Well, I thought you'd go with me," he said, nettled by her tone.

"What made you think that?" she asked coolly. "You have the sales list. It's your choice if you decide to buy."

"Yes, but—"

"You don't need me there," she went on, still irritated by his remarks about prestige. "I'm sure you can manage just fine by yourself." After all, she thought darkly; those are *your* kind of people, not mine.

"That's not the point!" he said, beginning to sound angry.

"What *is* the point, then?" she demanded impatiently.

"The point," he said heavily, "is that I'm asking you to go with me."

She couldn't help it; a thrill raced through her when he said that. She was about to relent when she realized that he just wanted her there in an advisory capacity; obviously it had nothing to do with the pleasure of her company—not the way he had said it. It had been more of an order than a request, and she lifted her chin defiantly. She wasn't going to be ordered around—not by him. She had done what he wanted by giving him that sales list; she had fulfilled her obligation, and she wasn't going to—

"I'm sorry," Jordan said before she could gather her angry thoughts. "I didn't mean that to sound like a—"

"Command?" Kendall supplied coldly. "Well, it did!"

He stiffened at that. "I said I was sorry!"

"So you did," she said, and turned away from him. She started toward the door, but he reached out and stopped her with a hand on her arm. This time she felt no tingle at the contact; she was still angry enough to jerk away.

"Kendall, wait. I said I was sorry, and I am. What I meant was, I'd like you to go to the sale with me. Please."

He hadn't given her an inch before; she refused to give him one now. "You don't need me there," she said, turning to face him again.

"No," he agreed quietly. "But I'd like you to be there with me all the same."

She looked up at him, wondering at this sudden change. She didn't know whether to believe him or not. She wanted to, but she still didn't trust him. Was all this apparent sincerity just an act?

Gazing into those dark eyes of his, Kendall knew she didn't care if it was. When he looked at her like that, she seemed to lose all resolve. She couldn't refuse him, but she still despised herself as she admitted defeat. "All right," she said ungraciously. "I'll go."

He smiled then, a slow smile that reached his eyes and crinkled the corners endearingly. Kendall felt her anger melting away. When he smiled like that, she could forget her suspicions and doubts about him; she could forget that he made her so angry, and that she always felt so awkward with him that she inevitably said the wrong thing. None of it mattered when he smiled, and she didn't care at that moment that she would regret her weakness.

"Thank you," he said simply, disarming her even more. "I'll pick you up. Unless"—he grinned this time, actually teasing her—"you want to drive yourself."

Now that she had made her decision, she felt suddenly lighthearted, almost gay, despite her doubts about him. Entering into the spirit of his teasing, she tossed her head. "Not that night," she said. "We're not going to take my old ranch truck when we can arrive in style!"

He laughed. "I'll be the chauffeur, then." His eyes twinkled as he added, "And we'll see if we can't make Kaylene Van Zandt poorer by one or two horses."

Kendall wasn't so sure about that. "If you buy even one of those horses, you'll be the one who's poorer, not Kaylene."

"We'll see about that," he said with supreme confidence.

Jordan watched Kendall drive away, thinking how small she looked behind the wheel of the truck, wondering why he always seemed to say the wrong thing to her. He hadn't felt this gauche since he was a teenager. What had happened to all the assured sophistication he had painstakingly developed over the years since then? She made him feel like a bumbling schoolboy, all hands and feet, stumbling over himself as if he hadn't learned a thing in thirty-five years. It was even worse that Martin had noticed it. Oh, he had seen the look in his friend's eyes, all right, and he would have said something to Martin if Kendall hadn't been there. He and Martin had been friends for a long time; he knew what Martin was thinking behind that bland expression—and he could have throttled him for it.

All right, so he was attracted to Kendall Voss; he admitted it. So what?

So what, indeed, he thought gloomily. He could be as attracted to her as he liked and it wouldn't get him anywhere. She had made it perfectly clear that she wasn't interested, so why couldn't he accept that? Was it just his ego trying to assert itself? He cringed at the thought, but he forced himself to examine it nevertheless. Maybe he was only interested in her because she insisted on being aloof from him. Maybe he was only attracted because she was unattainable. Maybe if she suddenly turned to him, he wouldn't be intrigued by her anymore. The grass was always greener, he reminded himself, and maybe . . .

Maybe, maybe, maybe. He was sick of all these ridiculous excuses he was making to himself. The simple fact was that he wanted her and she didn't want him. He should just accept that, as unpalatable as it was, and forget the whole thing. It was better this way, anyway. He had no business getting involved with a woman, especially one who clearly didn't want a man in her life.

Kendall hadn't said much about her husband that night at dinner, and he hadn't pressed her when he saw it was obvious that she didn't want to talk about him. He had understood that; he still couldn't talk about Marie, except to Martin. So he had respected Kendall's reticence. But now, remembering her face on that occasion, he wondered if he hadn't missed something important. He was sure that he had glimpsed a flash of angry contempt in her eyes when she mentioned her husband, and he wondered why. He could understand grief and guilt; God knows, he had suffered enough of that himself. But anger? Or contempt?

Maybe he should look into that more, he thought. He wasn't interested in gossip; he didn't care what kind of relationship Kendall had had with her husband, whoever he was. But there was something significant in her attitude, he was sure. And perhaps if he found out what it was, he'd understand her a little better.

At the least, he concluded glumly, he would know where he stood, and why.

Chapter 5

THE VAN ZANDT SALE WAS THE HIGHLIGHT OF THE WEEK. The huge pavilion that had been erected just for this night was packed hours before the auction even started, and by the time Kendall and Jordan arrived, the crowd was so dense that it was difficult even to get inside. Long buffet tables had been set up in a separate tent, and waiters stood behind them, serving everything from five different kinds of caviar to intricately decorated petits fours. Four chefs worked diligently at carving huge roasts and joints of every kind of meat, and the array of salads and platters of fruits was mind-boggling. A huge ice sculpture of a prancing horse dominated one of the tables, and champagne and fruit punch flowed from silver fountains.

The open bar at the other side of the tent was jammed, and the half-dozen bartenders rarely stopped for breath. Kendall smiled grimly at that sight; she knew as well as Kaylene did that well-lubricated buyers were the most aggressive—and often the most stubborn —in trying to outbid each other during the sale. She had seen it often—horses going for thousands of dollars more than they were worth simply because someone had had more than his share from the bar. She shrugged, knowing it was all part of the game, but wondering if Jordan recognized the ploy too.

"Some of these people are going to be pretty sorry in the morning, aren't they?" Jordan said, his lips close to her ear.

The din from the excited crowd was deafening; even with his head near hers, Kendall had to strain to hear him. Smiling, she was about to reply when she was suddenly lifted off her feet from behind. Wrapped in a bear hug, she couldn't see who had grabbed her, but she recognized the booming voice. "Kendall Voss! It's about time we saw you here!"

Kendall laughed as she was set on her feet again. Turning around, she faced the oilman who had been a friend of her father's for years. "Hello, George," she said, holding out her hand.

George Darling was a big man with a round, heavily jowled face and a paunch that had hidden his belt for longer than he could remember. He made no secret of the fact that he enjoyed his flamboyant lifestyle, and Kendall grinned when she saw the crimson shirt under his formal black, and the huge Stetson with the alligator hatband that matched his gargantuan boots. "I see you're in style, as always," she teased. "Don't tell me you came to buy another horse!"

"Heck no, darlin'," George boomed. "I came for the buffet!"

"All the way from Oklahoma? Don't tell me they don't feed you out there!"

"Well, Kaylene always did know how to put on a party."

"She certainly does," Kendall agreed dryly. She turned to Jordan then, introducing him. "Jordan, this is George Darling. George, Jordan Craig."

As the men shook hands, George asked, "Haven't seen you around here before, have I, Mr. Craig?"

"No, I just moved to Scottsdale."

"Well, I see you found the right person to show you around. This little lady knows just about all there is to know about those horses of ours, and if you want my advice, you'll listen to what she has to say. She and her daddy sold me my first Arab, started me on that little spread of mine. Isn't that right, darlin'?"

"George has about two hundred horses now," Kendall said to Jordan with a smile. "Hardly a little spread."

"Well, I do confess a fondness for the creatures," George said with a laugh. "Seems I never can sell 'em once they're on the place." He laughed again, a rich sound of such enjoyment that several people looked in their direction and laughed with him. "Thank the Lord I'm a better businessman than a horse breeder," George went on with a chuckle, "or the beasts would eat me out of house and home. Hey, I got some people to see, but maybe we can get together after the sale. Nice meeting you, Mr. Craig—and listen, if Kendall gives the nod to one of those horses up there tonight, you'd better buy it. She's got a better eye than even her daddy did—no disrespect intended, darlin'—and she won't steer you wrong!"

He was off then, moving through the crowd like a

huge tanker, scattering people with laughter and hearty slaps on unsuspecting backs. Kendall looked after him, grinning.

"He's a little overwhelming, isn't he?" she said to Jordan. "But I've never met a kinder, more generous person."

"He seems fond of you," Jordan commented.

"Oh, I've known him for years. In fact—"

But she never had a chance to finish what she'd been about to say. George Darling wasn't the only one who had noticed Kendall's presence tonight; for the next hour she was inundated with friends and acquaintances who came to talk to her, and in the confusion she barely had time to introduce Jordan before someone else came to greet her.

Finally a fanfare from the orchestra indicated the start of the auction, and they just had time to locate their reserved seats before the lights went down. In the expectant hush that followed, Jordan leaned close to her and said, "I didn't realize you were so popular. You seem to know everybody here—or if you don't, they certainly know you."

"That's because of my father," Kendall whispered back. "They remember him more than they do me."

"You're too modest, Kendall."

Too modest? No, she didn't think so. She knew these people better than he did. She had seen the speculation and curiosity in some of those eyes, and she knew what they were thinking. Oh, not everyone, of course; some of the greetings had been sincere, the pleasure at seeing her genuine. But there were always those who delighted in someone else's misfortune, especially if it enhanced their own chances of success, and there had been many of those here tonight. She had seen it in the covert glances tossed her way; she had felt it in the false heartiness of their handshakes and those sophisticated kisses that brushed air.

Perhaps she was being too sensitive, she told herself. Because she was still ashamed of the way Tony had dragged the Voss name through the mire, she could be seeing things that just weren't there. Besides, she had worked hard to right the wrongs Tony had done, and she couldn't be held accountable forever.

Couldn't she? People had long memories, selective memories that only remembered the bad things that had happened. With a sigh, she thought that she just might have to resign herself to those covert glances forever.

"Good evening, ladies and gentlemen!"

The announcer's voice, amplified by huge speakers set at intervals around the pavilion, broke into Kendall's thoughts. She looked up then to hear Kaylene Van Zandt being introduced, and when the lights went off dramatically again, she tried to prepare herself. Knowing Kaylene, her entrance would be spectacular.

It was. Silver spotlights highlighted Kaylene when she appeared on stage, and as she walked toward the center, the fog machines at floor level created a vapor that made it seem as if she were walking on clouds. Then the spotlights shifted to blues and greens except for the single cone of light that illuminated their hostess as she stood with her head bowed, acknowledging the applause of the crowd.

Kaylene was wearing a tight, long sheathlike gown of silver sequins that caught the light and threw it back into the audience, hurting the eyes. As always, she was wearing one of her elaborate platinum blond wigs, and tonight's choice was an outrageous affair of curls and waves that reached her shoulders. Even from where she was sitting, Kendall could see Kaylene's false eyelashes, so thick and long that she wondered how the woman could hold her eyes open. To another loud round of applause, in which Kendall joined halfheartedly, Kaylene lifted her head and smiled at the crowd. The announcer came forward to give her a microphone, and when she took it, her long nails gleamed crimson in the light.

How typical, Kendall thought with a disgusted sigh, and looked over at Jordan to see his reaction to the famous Kaylene Van Zandt. He was staring at her in complete bemusement as if he couldn't believe his eyes, and Kendall chuckled. He heard her laugh and tore his eyes away from the stage. "Is she for real?" he whispered.

"I'm afraid so," Kendall said wryly.

"Good Lord!" he said, awed.

After welcoming them all to her "extravaganza," Kaylene minced off the stage amid another tumultuous round of applause. The lights dimmed yet again, there was a long drum roll, another fanfare, and then suddenly, with a renewed blaze of light, the sale had begun.

Three hours later, Jordan himself was in the spotlight, the celebrated owner of all four of the horses Kendall had recommended to him. She stood dazedly beside him as he accepted congratulations from scores of well-wishers and owners anxious to meet the newcomer who had become an overnight sensation. Kendall was unable to believe what had happened.

He had been so cool, she thought. He had never betrayed by even the flicker of an eye if he was anxious or nervous as the prices climbed higher and higher; he just sat there, calmly outbidding everyone with a mere nod of his head. The spotters for the auctioneer had quickly discovered him, but strangely, there had been none of the friendly exhorting by the assistants that there had been when George Darling, for instance, had been bidding on a horse. Jordan, sitting quietly in his chair, legs casually crossed, one hand holding the program, had commanded respect just by his pose. He had been treated deferentially, recognized as a man who knew what he wanted, and who had already determined exactly how much he intended to pay. He seemed totally oblivious of the rubbernecking of the crowd as people strained to see who the newcomer was, and now that the sale was over, he was still in command. He looked completely at ease as he was introduced to some of the top breeders and owners in the business.

Standing in the background by her own choice, Kendall watched him and thought that he looked particularly handsome tonight in his evening clothes. Despite herself, she felt a thrill of pleasure at being with him; she hadn't missed the envious glances thrown her way by other women, and she was glad now that she had dipped into her meager funds to buy a new dress for the occasion. She knew that the icy green gown complemented her own coloring, and she had been so pleased at the effect that she hadn't even minded the outrageous price.

"Did I tell you how beautiful you look tonight?" Jordan whispered during a break in the conversation.

Kendall looked at him, startled. She hadn't thought he was even aware of her beside him; he had seemed so intent on acknowledging all the congratulations. But the look in his eyes told her that he was very aware of her indeed, and she flushed, pleased at the compliment.

"You look handsome yourself," she said. And then, without really being aware of what she was doing, she reached up to straighten his tie.

Their eyes met again, and suddenly the noise and confusion surrounding them faded away. It was as if they were alone in that vast place, and for a heart-stopping instant they just stared at each other. Kendall's heart began to pound, and it seemed as if she could hardly breathe. She felt the strength of his glance all through her, the power and the sheer compelling magnetism of him drawing her forward. Her lips trembled with the sudden desire that swept through her, and she couldn't look away from him. His eyes seemed almost black, and she saw herself, a tiny image in ice green, reflected in them. His lips parted, and, seemingly without volition, he started to bend his head toward her uplifted one. It was a magical moment, one she would always remember. She saw more than desire in his eyes, more than passion. She saw . . .

"Well, there you are!" a voice said, breaking the spell. "I've been looking all over for you!"

Kendall recognized the voice at once, and she turned in an instant rage toward its owner, on the point of screaming at her to go away. They had been so close, she thought furiously, *so close*. Now the moment was lost forever.

"Kaylene," she managed to say, summoning all her self-control. She absolutely would not make a scene, she told herself; Kaylene would enjoy it too much. She would be polite if it killed her.

A moment later, she thought it might. Kaylene

ignored her entirely, all her attention on Jordan as she
extended her manicured hand with its mammoth dia-
mond on one finger. "I'm Kaylene Van Zandt," she
purred.

"Jordan Craig," he said smoothly, hiding his instant
dislike of the woman. One look into those mascaraed
and heavily shadowed eyes told him that her appearance had been carefully calculated. She was not a
woman to be taken lightly, he thought, but he could
have cheerfully strangled her for interrupting at that
precise moment.

"Oh, I know who you are, Mr. Craig," Kaylene said.
"How could I not? You've made quite a splash at my
little sale tonight, you know. You've robbed me of four
of my best horses."

"Hardly a robbery," Jordan said dryly. "Unless, of
course, you consider it from my standpoint."

Kaylene put her hand coquettishly on his arm.
"Those animals are worth every penny you paid for
them, and you know it."

"Then we both came out ahead, didn't we?" he
replied suavely, resisting the urge to remove his arm
from her grasp. He turned to the silent Kendall, saying,
"You know Kendall Voss, of course."

Kaylene flicked a glance in Kendall's direction. "Of
course. We're old friends, aren't we, dear?"

Kendall didn't know how to answer that without
being rude, so she said nothing at all. It didn't seem to
matter; Kaylene had already dismissed her, turning
once again to Jordan.

"I'm having a little get-together tomorrow night,"
she said. "Just a few friends, to celebrate the sale. I'd
like you to come, Mr. Craig, since you seem to be one
of us now."

didn't want to explain. "Nothing's the matter. It's . . . it's been a long day, that's all."

"But—"

"Please, Jordan. I don't want to argue."

She started to walk away, but he wouldn't let her go that easily. Following her outside, he finally forced her to face him. "I thought you'd be pleased about tonight," he said.

"Why? Because you bought all four of those horses? Or because the great Kaylene Van Zandt came over herself to congratulate you?"

"So that's what this is about. You're angry about Kaylene."

"Don't be ridiculous!" she snapped. "I couldn't care less about that woman!"

"Oh, really? You don't sound like it."

"You can think what you like!"

"I don't know what to think, Kendall. I'd like to know why you're so angry."

"I'm not angry. I'm just tired. I want to go home. It's as simple as that."

"All right, then," he said, sounding angry now himself. "If that's what you want, we'll go!"

He took her arm then, steering her despite her protests to where they had left the car. He flung the door open and waited until she got in, then slammed the door again. After climbing in on the driver's side, he started the engine with a roar. Kendall sat stiffly, as far away from him as she could get, seething but determined not to say more. She was *not* going to talk about Kaylene; once she started, she wouldn't be able to stop.

They didn't speak for several minutes. Jordan was occupied with the traffic and didn't look at her, but after a covert glance in his direction, Kendall began to wish she hadn't made such a scene. She realized miserably that she had ruined what should have been a triumphant night for him, but every time she opened her mouth to say she was sorry, the words stuck in her throat. They were almost to her driveway before he said anything, and at his first words, her urge to apologize fled entirely.

"I'll drive tomorrow night," he said tightly. "Unless you prefer to take your own car and go alone."

"What are you talking about?" she snapped. "I'm not going anywhere tomorrow night!"

"Yes, you are. We're both committed to that party, and we're both going—separately or not!"

"I'm not going to Kaylene's party!" she said, outraged at the thought. *"You're* the one who accepted, not I!"

"The invitation included both of us, as I recall."

"Then you recall it wrong," Kendall retorted angrily. "I'm the last person in the world she'd invite anywhere, especially to one of her private little soirees! You may not have noticed," she added sarcastically, "but we're hardly on the best of terms. She ignored me the whole time, in fact. She was so busy making eyes at you that she didn't even notice I was there."

Jordan stopped the car in front of her house. He turned to look at her, and in the light from the porch she saw the hard glitter of his eyes. "Is that what this is all about?" he demanded. "You can't be jealous of Kaylene Van Zandt!"

"Jealous!" Kendall's voice rose an octave. "You must be out of your mind!"

"Why won't you go to that party, then?"

"I *told* you," Kendall said, gritting her teeth. "I

wasn't invited. But even if I had been, I still wouldn't go!"

"What are you afraid of?"

Now she was really furious. "I'm not afraid of anyone, especially her! But if you must know," she went on heedlessly, "I don't like that woman. I have never liked her, and I never will! I don't want anything to do with her and that . . . that crowd of hers!"

"Why not?"

If Jordan hadn't pressed her, she might have stopped right there. But his challenge banished the last of her self-control, and she answered furiously, "Because people like Kaylene use horses to show how powerful and important they are. It's all a game to them—to see who can put on the best show. They don't care about the horses themselves, and they certainly don't care about improving the breed! They'll promote inferior animals as superior individuals simply because they have the money to spend doing it! They get away with it, too, because they have the power and influence to see that it happens just like they planned. *That's* why I don't like her—and that's why I'm not going to that party!"

Jordan was silent for a moment after her outburst. She glared at him, daring him to contradict her. To her fury, he did.

"I don't think you're being fair. Breeders who can afford the best produce the best. It stands to reason, doesn't it?"

"Not if their chief interest is in seeing that certain horses bred by their select little group are the only ones promoted!"

Jordan was silent again, gazing at her thoughtfully. "Then we'll have to change that, won't we?"

Kendall's reply was scathing. "And just how do you propose to do that?"

"By going to that party, for starters," he said calmly. "Both of us."

"Oh, no you don't! I told you—"

He didn't wait for her to finish. He got out of the car and came around to open the door for her. She refused the offer of his hand, climbing out by herself and staring at him defiantly.

"I'm not going!" she said flatly.

"I'll pick you up at eight-thirty," he said firmly.

"I won't be here!"

"You'll be here."

"What makes you so sure?"

"Because you're a fighter. And this is important enough to fight for," he said calmly. "Good night, Kendall. It was . . . an evening I'll never forget."

Nor would she, Kendall fumed as she marched into the house, slamming the door behind her. Who did he think he was, anyway? She wasn't going to that stupid party; she wasn't. He could wait outside all night tomorrow for all she cared, but she absolutely, positively wasn't going.

Outside, Jordan sat in the car for a moment, staring at the door Kendall had closed with a bang. Reaching for a cigarette, he began to smile. What a temper she had! When she was angry, her eyes turned an even deeper green, a clear warning sign that she was about to let fly with both barrels. It was fascinating to watch, almost worth provoking her into an argument to see.

Kaylene better look to her defenses, he thought in amusement; that party tomorrow night was going to be even more interesting than she had promised. Kendall might be years younger than Kaylene, and less experienced in the ways of the world, but he would match her against the Van Zandt woman anytime. Yes, it was going to be interesting watching the sparks fly.

And maybe, he thought, smiling again, with a little careful planning on his part those sparks could be fanned into a flame.

Chapter 6

THE PARTY WAS A DISASTER, AS KENDALL HAD KNOWN IT would be. She hated herself for giving in and going with Jordan. All that day, until practically the last minute, she had told herself repeatedly that she was *not* going to be ready when he arrived. Then, a half hour before he was due, her chores all finished, the horses fed, the dishes done, and even her office straightened up, Kendall looked at herself in the mirror and knew she had to go. Racing around in all that frenetic activity hadn't been able to disguise the knowledge that, if she didn't, Jordan would be sure she was afraid of Kaylene. Having him believe that was worse than going to the damned party, so she marched upstairs in a fury to the shower.

By the time he arrived she was dressed in a simple white silk blouse and black crepe pants, knowing that Kaylene and her friends would be overdressed as usual,

apter 6

RTY WAS A DISASTER, AS KENDALL HAD KNOWN IT
e. She hated herself for giving in and going with
All that day, until practically the last minute,
told herself repeatedly that she was *not* going to
when he arrived. Then, a half hour before he
her chores all finished, the horses fed, the
ne, and even her office straightened up,
oked at herself in the mirror and knew she
. Racing around in all that frenetic activity
able to disguise the knowledge that, if she
dan would be sure she was afraid of Kaylene.
believe that was worse than going to the
ty, so she marched upstairs in a fury to the

ne he arrived she was dressed in a simple
ouse and black crepe pants, knowing that
her friends would be overdressed as usual

wasn't invited. But even if I had been, I still wouldn't
go!"

"What are you afraid of?"

Now she was really furious. "I'm not afraid of
anyone, especially her! But if you must know," she
went on heedlessly, "I don't like that woman. I have
never liked her, and I never will! I don't want anything
to do with her and that . . . that crowd of hers!"

"Why not?"

If Jordan hadn't pressed her, she might have stopped
right there. But his challenge banished the last of her
self-control, and she answered furiously, "Because
people like Kaylene use horses to show how powerful
and important they are. It's all a game to them—to see
who can put on the best show. They don't care about
the horses themselves, and they certainly don't care
about improving the breed! They'll promote inferior
animals as superior individuals simply because they
have the money to spend doing it! They get away with
it, too, because they have the power and influence to
see that it happens just like they planned. *That's* why I
don't like her—and that's why I'm not going to that
party!"

Jordan was silent for a moment after her outburst.
She glared at him, daring him to contradict her. To her
fury, he did.

"I don't think you're being fair. Breeders who can
afford the best produce the best. It stands to reason,
doesn't it?"

"Not if their chief interest is in seeing that certain
horses bred by their select little group are the only ones
promoted!"

Jordan was silent again, gazing at her thoughtfully.
"Then we'll have to change that, won't we?"

Kendall's reply was scathing. "And just how do you propose to do that?"

"By going to that party, for starters," he said calmly. "Both of us."

"Oh, no you don't! I told you—"

He didn't wait for her to finish. He got out of the car and came around to open the door for her. She refused the offer of his hand, climbing out by herself and staring at him defiantly.

"I'm not going!" she said flatly.

"I'll pick you up at eight-thirty," he said firmly.

"I won't be here!"

"You'll be here."

"What makes you so sure?"

"Because you're a fighter. And this is important enough to fight for," he said calmly. "Good night, Kendall. It was . . . an evening I'll never forget."

Nor would she, Kendall fumed as she marched into the house, slamming the door behind her. Who did he think he was, anyway? She wasn't going to that stupid party; she wasn't. He could wait outside all night tomorrow for all she cared, but she absolutely, positively wasn't going.

Outside, Jordan sat in the car for a moment, staring at the door Kendall had closed with a bang. Reaching for a cigarette, he began to smile. What a temper she had! When she was angry, her eyes turned an even deeper green, a clear warning sign that she was about to let fly with both barrels. It was fascinating to watch, almost worth provoking her into an argument to see.

Kaylene better look to her defenses, he thought in amusement; that party tomorrow night was going to be even more interesting than she had promised. Kendall

Ch

THE PA
would
Jordan.
she had
be ready
was due
dishes d
Kendall l
had to go
hadn't bee
didn't, Jor
Having hir
damned pa
shower.
By the tir
white silk bl
Kaylene and
98

and hoping that she would look deliberately under-
stated by contrast. When she opened the door and saw
the look of admiration on Jordan's face, she refused to
be pleased by it, or flattered by the compliment he gave
her about the way she looked.

She still wasn't ready to forgive him for the quarrel
last night, so she was cool and distant on the drive over,
just waiting for him to comment on her capitulation.
He didn't. As if he sensed that she was looking for an
excuse to quarrel again, he talked of inconsequential
things the whole time, and Kendall was reduced to
answering in monosyllables as revenge.

"Are we going to keep this up the whole night?"
Jordan asked as they were walking up the steps toward
Kaylene's elaborate front door.

"I haven't the faintest idea what you mean," Kendall
said haughtily, refusing to look at him.

"You know very well what I mean," Jordan said in
exasperation. "You haven't said two words since I
picked you up."

"I didn't think you'd be interested in anything I had
to say. You certainly weren't last night."

"That's not true."

"Isn't it?" She whirled to face him, hoping to get this
over with before someone opened the door. "I *told* you
I didn't want to come tonight, but oh, no! You insisted.
You knew better! So here I am. I did what you wanted.
Just don't expect me to be happy about it!"

Jordan stared at her for a moment. Then, to her
amazement, he began to smile.

"What's so funny?" she demanded hotly.

He shook his head. "I know it sounds trite, but do
you realize how beautiful you are when you're angry?"

"*What!*"

"You are, you know."

"I don't believe this!" she sputtered. "How can you stand there and . . . and . . . ."

She never had a chance to finish. Before she realized what he was doing, he had taken her into his arms and started to kiss her.

Kendall uttered an outraged cry, but his mouth was hard on hers, and her struggle was only token, almost nonexistent. She made a feeble attempt to push him away, then gave up the effort entirely, lost in an instant to the sensation of his lips on hers. Her arms went around him of their own volition, and when he pulled her tightly into him, she felt herself straining to be even closer to that hard body that was suddenly trembling as much as her own.

Neither of them heard anyone approach the door from the other side. When it was suddenly thrown open and they were pinned in the spill of light from the entry, they both looked up dazedly, still wrapped in each other's arms.

"I thought I heard someone out here," Kaylene said with sly amusement.

Kendall jumped back from Jordan, feeling her face turn crimson with embarrassment. She dared a quick look in his direction, fighting the impulse to straighten her blouse or run a hand through her hair, feeling completely disheveled and bemused. She didn't know what to say; she was so mortified that she couldn't even speak.

Jordan didn't seem the least embarrassed. Hardly missing a beat, he turned to their hostess and said, "Good evening, Kaylene."

One eyebrow raised, Kaylene smiled. To Kendall's

humiliation, her glance swept them both speculatively and Kendall forced herself to meet the other woman's eyes. She realized then that Kaylene had known they were on the doorstep and had waited for just this moment before opening the door. She must have been watching the whole time, Kendall thought furiously. She must have been. Kaylene had an army of servants; she never answered the door herself.

"Please come in," Kaylene said, while Kendall fought for control. "It's delightful seeing you again, Jordan—and you, too, my dear. How nice of you to come."

Kendall felt Kaylene's eyes on her as she preceded Jordan inside, and she wished that somehow she could just disappear. She wanted to run away from that look on Kaylene's face, but it was too late. She was here now; she would just have to hold her head up and act as if nothing had happened.

Nothing *had* happened, she told herself fiercely. It wasn't a crime to kiss someone, was it? But she knew from Kaylene's expression what the woman was thinking, and she squirmed inwardly, knowing how Kaylene would interpret the scene. She could just imagine her now, murmuring to her cronies; "Oh yes, I caught them *kissing* on the front steps, if you can imagine."

There would be titterings and sly chuckles and solemn shakings of heads, and then someone—probably Kaylene herself, Kendall thought blackly—would say; "Well, of course she's after his money. She has to be desperate now, after that debacle with her husband last year. I do think someone should warn him . . . don't you?"

Gritting her teeth at this imagined scenario, Kendall

took one look into the crowded living room and wondered how she was going to get through the evening.

"You don't mind if I spirit Jordan away, do you, dear?" Kaylene said at her elbow. "You know most of the people here, I believe—and it's unfair for you to monopolize such a handsome, *eligible* man."

Kendall looked into Kaylene's glittering eyes and resisted the urge to tear the platinum wig from her head. "Please do," she said coolly, making a supreme effort to control herself. "I can manage by myself. I have for quite a while now, you know."

The green-shadowed eyes narrowed. "A situation you'd no doubt like to change," Kaylene purred. "But don't you think he's a little out of your league?"

Before Kendall could answer, Kaylene moved away. Taking Jordan's arm, she began moving about the room while Kendall stood there clenching her fists in impotent rage. A little out of her league! Maybe what Kaylene had really meant was that he obviously belonged in hers. She'd had five husbands already. Had she set her sights on a sixth? Gritting her teeth again at the thought, Kendall took a glass of champagne from a passing waiter and drank it in one gulp.

"Why, Kendall, what a surprise to see you here!"

Kendall turned at the sound of the voice beside her, recognizing the speaker with instant pleasure. The little man at her elbow was Edgar Hamlin, one of the top industrialists in the country. White-haired and bespectacled, he looked more like a kindly old grandfather than a shrewd, almost ruthless businessman—an image reinforced by the fact that the top of his head barely reached her shoulder. She had known him for years, their common ground being an avid interest in the Arabian horse.

"How are you, Mr. Hamlin?" she asked with a smile.

"Bored to tears, if you want to know the truth. I don't know why I let Kaylene talk me into coming to these parties of hers. It's always the same old thing, every one of them trying to outtalk everyone else."

Kendall's smile broadened. Despite his complaint, she suspected that Edgar really enjoyed these parties during Scottsdale Week. He was a sought-after guest, not only because of his wealth and stable of fine horses, but because he was witty and amusing. Kendall could listen to his stories for hours, and as a child she often had.

"They're all just jealous," she said solemnly, hiding her amusement. "You've had more national champions and top-ten horses than all these people put together."

"Oh, I don't know about that . . . ," he said deprecatingly, looking at her from under his white brows.

"I do."

Edgar smiled back at her. "That's what I always liked about you, Kendall. Even as a youngster, you always spoke your piece. People don't do that very often around me. Can't imagine why."

"I can," Kendall said dryly, knowing very well that he knew exactly why people hesitated to tell him things he might not want to hear.

He laughed. "We've known each other too long for false modesty, haven't we?" he said, and then looked across the room to where Jordan stood, surrounded by a knot of people. "Isn't that the young man who bought Kaylene's best horses last night?"

Kendall nodded, gazing at Jordan herself. He was so

tall that he was almost a head above any of the group that surrounded him, and his lean profile stood out in sharp contrast to Kaylene's friends, who were beginning to sport heavy jowls and increasing paunches. "Yes. His name is Jordan Craig."

"Craig . . . I've heard of him before," Edgar said thoughtfully. "Now, where . . . . Yes, I remember now. He was involved in some car accident last year; that was it."

Kendall looked at Edgar in shocked surprise. "He mentioned something about his wife dying in an accident," she said. "But he never said anything about being involved himself."

"Well, he nearly died too, as I recall. Terrible thing. It was in all the papers." He glanced at her. "Your Mr. Craig is a unique man, Kendall, but I imagine you know that."

Kendall stirred. "He's not my Mr. Craig," she protested, too vehemently. "He's just a—a client."

Edgar smiled knowingly, and, despite herself, Kendall flushed. They were interrupted just then by several men who bore Edgar away, anxious for his advice about the stock market. Kendall paid little attention to the scraps of conversation floating back to her about margins and points; she was too dismayed by the look she had seen in Hamlin's sharp blue eyes. Was it so obvious how she felt about Jordan? she wondered, appalled.

Retreating to a corner of the room, she thought about what Edgar had said about the car accident. Jordan hadn't mentioned that he'd been in the car too, she thought, remembering that night at dinner. But she knew Edgar well enough to know that he hadn't made a mistake; he was too well informed about too many things.

Her eyes sought Jordan again, and she frowned. It seemed obvious now that he was still suffering the aftereffects of that accident—both emotionally and physically. She recalled with a pang how stiffly he had walked that first day, how worried she had been that he had hurt himself helping her with the pipe. She also remembered those times when he had abruptly withdrawn, as if she had said something that offended him or caused him pain. Thoughtfully she gazed at him, and understood why. She knew how long it had taken her to get over Tony's death, and even more over the way he had died. And she hadn't even been directly involved. It must be so much worse for Jordan to have been there, to have almost died himself.

Jordan looked up just then, and their eyes met. He stared at her for a long moment, then abruptly excused himself to the people he was with. As he walked across the room toward her, Kendall was unable to take her eyes off him. He was so handsome, she thought, so sure of himself. It was an irresistible combination, and every time she looked at him she felt that stirring inside her. Remembering the quick fire of his kiss, she felt suddenly weak with longing. She didn't care that he was still full of remorse over the loss of his wife, or that he might not ever get over her death. She didn't care that his lifestyle was so different from hers, or that their opinions rarely concurred. She wanted him in that moment; she wanted him—desperately and without reservation—for an instant, or a night . . . or a lifetime.

I'm in love with him, she thought wonderingly. I

don't know anything about him, really, but I don't care. What am I going to do?

"Why didn't you rescue me?" Jordan said as he came up to her. "I thought I was going to have to talk business all night."

"You looked like you were holding your own," Kendall replied, hoping that her expression didn't betray her. She needed time to think, time to decide what she was going to do—or if she was going to do anything at all—about this emotional quandary she'd suddenly found herself in.

"So did you. That was Edgar Hamlin you were talking to, wasn't it? You constantly surprise me, Kendall."

"Why is that?" She was having a difficult time keeping track of the conversation. Too aware of his arm against hers, she felt the pounding of her heart at that casual contact and despaired. How could she disguise her feelings for him when the slightest touch made her tremble?

"You seem to know so many important people—from every walk of life."

Kendall forced a laugh. "That's what he said about you."

Jordan raised an eyebrow. "I've never even met the man."

"Well, he knows who you are. Would you like to meet him? He's really very nice—like a kindly old grandfather."

The eyebrow went even higher at that. "Only you would say a thing like that," he said, amused. "From what I hear, Edgar Hamlin is an absolute tyrant in the boardroom. He runs that company with an iron fist and always has."

Now was her chance to find out something about him, Kendall thought. "What about you?" she asked as casually as she could. "I imagine you can be something of a tyrant yourself. Or does Craig Industries run itself?"

Something flickered in Jordan's eyes, and Kendall realized despairingly that she had trod on that private ground again. "It has this past year, I'm afraid," Jordan said, his voice cool. "Fortunately, my executive officers are capable men. More than I can say for their president these past months."

Kendall heard the bitterness in those last words and wished she hadn't said anything at all. "Jordan, I—"

But just then, with her uncanny sense of timing, their hostess materialized again at her elbow. Kendall wanted to scream. Kaylene seemed to have an unerring knack for interrupting them at important moments, and Kendall was sure that she'd been listening and waiting for her opportunity.

"Kendall, you really mustn't monopolize Jordan," Kaylene admonished, shaking a playful finger in Kendall's face.

Kendall decided to fight fire with fire. "I'm sorry, Kaylene," she said innocently. "I was just telling Jordan about my conversation with Edgar."

Kaylene's eyes narrowed at that; she had never wanted to acknowledge that Edgar Hamlin, and others like him, were fond of Kendall and that she knew them perhaps better than Kaylene did herself.

"Yes," Kaylene said, the glitter of malice in her eyes, "I saw you talking to him. A social setting is such an opportunity, isn't it?"

Kendall held on to her temper with an effort. "An opportunity for what?"

"Why, to ask his help, of course," Kaylene said sweetly. "I mean, your situation . . . ." She allowed her voice to trail away, glancing quickly at Jordan to make sure he got the point.

Kendall knew that Jordan hadn't missed anything. "My situation, as you call it," she said sharply, "is no one's business but my own!"

"Oh, of course, I couldn't agree more," Kaylene said, still using that honeyed tone. She turned appealingly to Jordan. "It's just that we all think Kendall is so brave, you know. If *my* husband had done what Tony did, well . . . I'm sure I would have been crushed, just crushed. And yet this dear girl carries on as if nothing had happened. I do admire that, don't you?"

"Kendall has many admirable qualities," Jordan said smoothly. "I can't imagine her being crushed by anything."

Kendall shot him a surprised glance, but Kaylene wasn't finished yet. "She does indeed," she said, abandoning her sympathetic pretense in irritation. "Unfortunately, though, common sense doesn't seem to be one of them. I'm sorry, Kendall, but you know it's true. If it wasn't, you would have sold me that mare of yours when I offered to buy her."

Kendall should have known that Kaylene would use this opportunity to make some remark about Cantata. She knew that her refusal to part with the mare still rankled with Kaylene, who hated to be thwarted in anything. She was about to make an angry reply when Jordan spoke.

"What mare is that?" he asked.

"She means Cantata," Kendall said curtly. "But she knows that nothing will make me sell that mare, whatever the offer."

"You'll change your mind," Kaylene said with arrogant assurance. "You'll have to, sooner or later, I'm sure. And I did make you a generous offer; even you have to admit that. Of course," she said to Jordan as Kendall stood there seething, "it's not as if I really *need* that mare. I was only trying to help."

Kendall managed to hold on to her self-control until they were finally in the car and on the way home. The hour following that conversation with Kaylene had been endless, a trial of endurance in which she smiled and chatted with the few guests who approached her— and who, like Edgar Hamlin, had been too polite or too fond of her to mention either Tony or the damage he had done to her reputation. But she had seen speculation in other eyes, and it was all she could do to hold her head high and ignore it. She knew what those people were thinking, and with every passing minute her bitterness and sense of futility increased. Even if she managed to pay off all the debts Tony had left behind, would she ever be able to restore her name— or, more importantly, that of Voss Arabians? Judging from the sly glances she had intercepted all evening, she began to doubt it.

The men and women at the party were some of the most influential and powerful in the horse world; worse, most of them were devoted to Kaylene. They were all cut from the same cloth and under her influence; a word from any of them could destroy Kendall despite how hard she worked to establish herself again. It was no concern of theirs that Tony had done what he had without her knowledge; she had been his wife and was therefore equally responsible, no matter how unfair or unjust it seemed to blame her.

And it *was* unfair, Kendall thought angrily. Even

knowing that men like Edgar would come to her
defense couldn't completely eradicate the humiliation
she had endured that night, and by the time she and
Jordan finally left, she was almost in tears.

"I'm sorry I insisted that you come with me," Jordan
said after a long silence.

"It's a little late for that, isn't it?" Kendall said
bitterly.

"Well, I thought that if you made an appearance—"

Kendall's temper, so close to the surface all evening,
flared now. She had endured too much, felt too humiliated for too long, to contain her anger at the injustice
of it all now. She looked across the car at him furiously.
"You thought! You *thought!* What do you know about
it, anyway? All you can think of is how pleased you are
that Kaylene Van Zandt is so eager to include you in
that crowd of hers! Well, congratulations, Mr. Craig—
you've done it! You're a full-fledged member of the
group. You can swagger around like the rest of them
now, pretending you're a horse breeder just like they
do!"

Jordan gripped the steering wheel tightly, trying to
control himself. "Is that what you think? That I want to
be like that?"

"Well, you certainly acted like it tonight!"

"How was I supposed to act? Did you want me to
stand in a corner and sulk all night—like you did?"

"I didn't sulk!" Kendall cried, outraged.

"What do you call it, then?"

"You don't understand!"

"I think I do." He looked across at her. "Look,
Kendall, just because your husband pulled some shady
deals doesn't mean—" He stopped, alerted by her

expression. She had tensed, staring at him with a look of disbelief, but he had realized his mistake too late.

"How did you find out?" she asked, her lips stiff.

"Well . . . it seems obvious that it was something like that, just from what Kaylene said," he answered lamely, reluctant to confess how much he knew, or how he had found out.

"It isn't just what Kaylene said, is it?" Kendall demanded. Her voice rose shrilly, but she didn't care. "You've been poking around, haven't you? Prying into my private affairs!"

"No."

"You have! How else would you know about Tony? Oh, you certainly are in good company with Kaylene and her crowd, aren't you?" she said bitterly. "Was that why you insisted that I come with you tonight? So that you could all gloat?"

"That isn't fair!" Jordan said sharply.

"Fair! Don't talk to me about fair!" she cried. "Oh, I should have known you'd be on her side!"

"I'm not on her side!"

"What do you call it, then?"

"If I'm on anyone's side, it's yours," Jordan said, too infuriated now at her stubbornness to think about what he was saying. Some small voice inside him warned him to be careful, but in his anger and impatience he went too far. "Why do you think I asked you to be my agent?" he demanded, and then went on heedlessly without waiting for her to answer. "I wanted to help you, Kendall, though God knows why! You're so damned proud; you're sure you can do it all by yourself. Maybe I should have let you try!"

"Maybe you should have!" Kendall cried, outraged.

"I was doing just fine without you! I don't need you or anyone else to help me, and if you concocted this agent business out of some misguided Good Samaritan impulse, I don't want any part of it. I resign!"

"Just like that? We have an agreement, remember?"

They were shouting at each other, sitting in the car outside her front door. Kendall didn't even remember getting there, but she was glad they had. She reached for the door handle and flung herself out of the car, slamming the door as hard as she could.

Jordan didn't try to stop her. His jaw tight, he watched her run up the steps. As she disappeared into the house, he banged his hand against the steering wheel in a gesture of impotent rage. He had never met a woman as stubborn and proud and . . . and deliberately obstinate as Kendall Voss, he thought furiously, and he was glad this had happened. As far as he was concerned, it was all over between them. Finished. The end.

Kendall reached her bedroom before she began to cry. Tears running down her face, she stood in the middle of the room, her hands clenched. She had never felt so humiliated in her life as when he'd said that all he wanted to do was help her. Help her! She now knew that the only reason for all this attention from him was because he pitied her. *Pitied her.*

Cringing at the thought, she dashed the tears away with her hand. She never wanted to see him again, she thought furiously. Never! She didn't need pity from anyone, especially him. He and Kaylene and that whole crowd could laugh up their sleeves at her; she didn't care. She had come this far without anyone's help; she'd go on without it, too.

And as soon as Cantata had her foal, she thought savagely, she'd be the one laughing. Cantata was her last ace, but with a mare like that, one ace was all she needed. Then she'd show them—show them all, including the high-and-mighty Jordan Craig!

Oh, she hated him. She hated him! How could she ever have imagined herself in love with a man like that? It was ludicrous, insane! Remembering her thoughts about him tonight at the party, she cringed. If she had confessed . . . if he had found out how she felt . . . she never would have been able to hold her head up again.

She was glad this had happened. She must have been out of her mind to imagine even for an instant that she wanted him. Wanted him! She never wanted to see the man again!

Chapter 7

KENDALL WAS OUT IN THE BARN EARLY THE NEXT MORN-
ing, working with feverish energy in an attempt to
convince herself that she wasn't exhausted from an
almost sleepless night. She had awakened at dawn, still
in the grip of dreams in which Jordan had been the
predominant figure. Thinking about it now, she felt her
face grow hot with shame. In her dreams, she and
Jordan had been lovers, and she could still recall too
vividly the heights of passion she had experienced with
him in fantasy.

Disgusted with herself, she worked harder than ever,
finishing the stall cleaning in record time, trying to
drive out all thoughts of him. It didn't work. She could
see him in her mind's eye at the party last night, a head
above any man there, his eyes searching her out from
the other side of the room. She paused finally, leaning
on the rake, her eyes closed in pain.

She couldn't forget him, she thought. As angry as she had been with him last night, the idea of never seeing him again desolated her.

"Kendall?"

As if her thoughts had conjured him up, Jordan was standing there when she opened her eyes. He was silhouetted in the light from the doorway, and at the sight of him her heart gave a painful lurch. She couldn't speak; she just stood there staring at him as he walked slowly toward her, almost hesitant to approach.

"Kendall, I came to say . . . I'm sorry about last night."

Still she couldn't speak. Her mouth was so dry that she couldn't have said anything even if she'd known what to say.

He came closer, and in the light that filtered down from the skylights, she saw the dark circles under his eyes and thought disbelievingly that he hadn't slept well either.

"I don't want to fight over a silly woman like Kaylene," he went on when she remained silent. A wry smile flitted across his face, and he added, "Especially when there are so many other things to argue about." The smile disappeared, and he looked at her somberly. "Did you really mean it when you said you quit as my agent?" he asked quietly.

Kendall found her tongue at last. "I did last night."

"And now?"

She shook her head slowly, unable to lie to him. "I was angry last night. I thought . . . Oh, it doesn't matter what I thought. I'm sorry too."

The rake clattered to the ground as he held out his arms. Kendall rushed into his embrace, lifting her head to stare up at him. "Jordan . . ."

He pulled her to him, kissing her fiercely. She responded with a fierceness of her own, wondering how she could ever have imagined forgetting him. Breathing in the scent of him, reveling in the taste of his lips, she felt alive again—alive with the passion and desire she had tried to deny. He was like a rainfall after a drought; she could almost feel herself blossoming in his embrace.

He held her so tightly that she could hardly breathe. She didn't care. It was blissful being held by him, molding her body to his, all her senses swimming with the sensation of being in his arms, of his seeking mouth on hers. The pounding of her heart was like a drum roll in her ears, and she didn't care if the world came to an end right then. He had come back to her, and this instant was all that mattered. She wanted this moment to go on forever.

"Kendall?"

The precious moment was shattered abruptly. They both looked up, and when Kendall saw Dennis Atchison there, she sprang away from Jordan and faced Dennis with her hands clenched.

"What are you doing here?" she demanded. She was aware that Jordan had stepped slightly away from her, too, and she sensed that he was just as irate as she was at the interruption. She could almost feel the dislike emanating from him, and she wanted to say that she hadn't planned this. She couldn't look at him; all her attention was focused on Dennis, willing him to leave before he made a scene. From the look on his face, she knew that making a scene was exactly what he intended to do, and she knew from experience how childish he could be. If she'd been able to, she would have thrown him out bodily before he did any

more harm. Why had he chosen *this* moment to come
here? In another moment she and Jordan would
have . . .

"I didn't realize you . . . ah . . . had company,"
Dennis said, actually swaggering toward them, his
hands stuck in his pockets.

Kendall hadn't missed the sarcastic tone of his voice
—nor the jealous expression in his eyes as he came
forward. She was even more irritated at that, thinking
that he had no right to feel possessive. He didn't have a
right to be here at all. She had told him that she didn't
want to see him; she had asked—demanded—that he
leave her alone.

She was about to tell him again, more forcefully this
time if she had to, when Dennis stuck his hand out.
"I'm Dennis Atchison," he said, as if the name should
automatically mean something to Jordan.

Jordan nodded perfunctorily. "Jordan Craig."

"I know who you are," Dennis said. He had lowered
his voice to match Jordan's deeper register, and if
Kendall hadn't been so annoyed at the situation she
would have laughed. What a fool Dennis was, she
thought contemptuously. As if he could possibly match
Jordan in anything!

"Oh?" Jordan said indifferently.

Dennis jutted his jaw out. "Yeah—I just passed your
place. You're doing a lot of work there for nothing, Mr.
Craig. You're never going to get what you want," he
said, flashing a triumphant look in Kendall's direction.
"Not while I'm around, anyway."

Kendall couldn't believe that even Dennis would say
such a thing. She gaped at him, wondering what was
wrong with him. Didn't he realize that he was making a
complete fool of himself?

Jordan seemed amused. "Oh? And just what is it that you think I want?"

Dennis's eyes narrowed. He'd heard the amusement in Jordan's tone and he didn't like it. "Well, for starters," he said, "I've heard that you're after Kendall's property. And it seems pretty obvious now just how you're going to go about getting it."

"Dennis!" Kendall said, outraged.

"Let me handle this," Jordan said, beginning to sound angry himself.

She glanced at him. "But—"

"I want you to know something, Mr. Jordan Craig," Dennis said, ignoring Kendall's protest. "You might have fooled Kendall with all your sweet talk, but you don't fool me. Kendall is my girl, and you'd better stay away from her."

"Now just a minute, Dennis!" Kendall began furiously. "I'm not—"

"Kendall is a grown woman," Jordan said evenly, ignoring her as he glared at the other man. "She can make up her own mind."

"Oh, is that so?" Dennis sneered. "I have to admit you're pretty clever, buying all those fancy horses and boarding them here. But even if she doesn't see through you, I do. And you're not going to get away with it."

Jordan took a step forward. "Is that some kind of threat?"

Despite himself, Dennis took a step back. "You take it any way you want!" he said belligerently.

I don't believe this, Kendall thought, staring at the two men as they glowered at each other. It was like some bad television movie where the woman was supposed to stand meekly aside while two men fought for possession. Dennis saying that she was his girl—his *girl,* for God's sake—and Jordan saying, "I'll handle this, Kendall," as if she couldn't speak for herself. Who did they think they were, anyway? Who did they think *she* was? It was time they both found out.

"I'd appreciate it if you wouldn't act like I'm not even here," she said angrily as she stepped between the two men. "I can speak for myself."

They both looked blankly at her, and she nearly laughed at their almost identical expressions. It was as if they *had* forgotten that she was there, and that irritated her even more. "I think you'd both better leave," she said. "I don't have time for this childishness. I've got work to do."

Jordan's eyes darkened at that. He started to say something, but the look on her face stopped him. His jaw tight, he said, "You're right. I don't have time for it either. It seems we have different . . . priorities, doesn't it?"

He brushed by her then, walking away without looking back. Kendall stiffened, wondering what he had meant but too proud to call him back to ask him. Different priorities? Well, perhaps they did, she thought, tossing her head. He obviously thought that things were fine only if they were going his way—that she had no right to an opinion if it differed from his. Well, if that was the way he felt, she wasn't going to beg him to stay and explain; she had *priorities* too.

And one of them was putting Dennis in his place. He was staring after Jordan with a satisfied smile on his face, but before he could turn to her again, she said, "I hope you're pleased with yourself, Dennis. You acted like a complete fool."

"Now, wait a minute—"

"No, *you* wait! I meant it when I told you to leave. I meant it when I said I didn't want you to come here anymore, and when I told you I didn't want you to call. I'm *not* your girl; I never was. When are you going to get that through your head?"

Dennis's face had reddened. "So I was right," he said nastily. "That guy's got your head all turned around."

"Jordan has nothing to do with this!"

"Oh, doesn't he?" Dennis sneered. "It looks to me like you've been taken in again. I thought you learned something after Tony, but I guess not. Or don't you remember what a smooth-talker he was, too?"

When Dennis had gone, angrily gunning his motor and leaving in a spray of gravel, Kendall went into the house. It was long past lunchtime, but she had no appetite after that scene in the barn. She took a can of soda from the refrigerator and plopped into a kitchen chair, then sat glumly staring at the stack of unpaid bills she had left on the table.

Damn Dennis anyway, she thought resentfully. If he hadn't shown up, none of this would have happened. She and Jordan would have become lovers; she knew it. She couldn't have stopped it; she wouldn't have. She had been so aroused by that single kiss that nothing else would have mattered. Remembering the smoothness of his lips and the feel of his hands on her, Kendall felt flushed. Her body ached for his; she felt restless and dissatisfied, burning with longing. She had wanted him so badly that she hadn't thought about anything else. They could have made love right there in the barn and she wouldn't have cared.

And after that? What would have happened after that?

Kendall stood up restlessly. She walked over to the window and gazed out at Jordan's mares that she had put in the pasture for exercise this morning. But as she stared at them, she heard Dennis's ugly accusations again, and she frowned.

"You're pretty clever, buying all those fancy horses and boarding them here. . . ."

Was it all part of a game Jordan was playing? Was Dennis right about that much, at least? Jordan had asked if she would also board the horses he had bought at the sale, and she had said yes. Was that another part of the plan? Was she supposed to be so dazzled by all this attention that she failed to see what he was really after? *Did* he want to buy her ranch and add it to his own? She frowned again, then drank the last of her soda before tossing the can into the wastebasket.

She didn't know what to think anymore. She was so attracted to him that when he was near she couldn't think of anything else but him. All the questions that plagued her when she was alone vanished like smoke when she was with him; the sheer power of his presence obliterated all other considerations.

She was acting like a silly teenager with a crush, she thought disgustedly, and it had to stop. If she wanted a clear indication of how Jordan felt, she couldn't have a better example than when he had walked away from her with that remark about priorities. If he had really cared, he would have stayed, she thought angrily. They could at least have talked about it; he could have told her how he felt. But he hadn't stayed, and he obviously didn't want her to know how he felt, and wasn't that the most telling indication of all?

Instead of hating Dennis for interrupting them when

he did, she should be grateful that he had. However that scene had turned out, at least it saved her from making an even bigger fool of herself than she had already. If she and Jordan had become lovers, would he just have accomplished one more objective? Was that just another part of the plan to disarm her to the point where she wouldn't be able to refuse him anything?

She had to face it, she told herself; she had to admit that he'd been playing a game all along. She had seen how easily he fit in with Kaylene and her crowd; she knew he was more than equal to any of those people. He had spent a fortune for those horses without batting an eye, and he was building a showplace for them that would rival any in the area. So why would he be interested in her? He wasn't, she thought bleakly. He never had been, except as a tool to help him get what he wanted. As Dennis had cruelly pointed out, she had been so wrong about Tony. It seemed now that she had been blinded by Jordan, as well.

But not anymore, she told herself fiercely. Not anymore.

Depressed by her thoughts, Kendall wandered back to the table. The stack of bills and her unopened mail still lay there, and with a heavy sigh, she sat down. She was glancing indifferently through the morning's delivery when an envelope caught her eye. Recognizing the logo in the left corner, she opened the envelope to see a sales list from a ranch in Idaho. It was a dispersal sale, and she was about to throw the paper away, when a name on the list caught her eye. Surprised, she stared at it. Usually a dispersal meant that the owner was getting rid of inferior stock or selling those animals that hadn't contributed much to the breeding program. But one of the horses on this list was by no means inferior. In fact, she thought with rising excitement, the young stallion listed here would be perfect for Jordan's own program. It was an opportunity too good for him to miss, and she was reaching eagerly for the phone when she snatched her hand back.

She must be out of her mind to think of calling him after what had happened this morning. Jordan had stalked out of here less than an hour ago, and she had spent the time since then telling herself that she was glad he had. It would be insane to call him now; if she did, she'd only get involved again, and that was precisely what she had promised herself she'd avoid. It was best to leave things as they were; she knew it was. She was certain of it.

Except that she still had his horses here, she reminded herself glumly. She had to talk to him sometime; she couldn't just ignore the fact that she was responsible for his animals, and that four more were going to be under her care. What was she going to do about that?

She couldn't deal with that question right now; she had to face it another time. But her glance kept straying to the dispersal list in her hand, and finally she crumpled it into a tight ball and threw it away with a gesture of finality. Jordan could find his own horses from now on, she thought defiantly. It was no longer any concern of hers. Resolutely, she pulled the stack of bills toward her and plunged in.

The phone rang that night just as Kendall was coming in from evening chores. It had rung on and off all afternoon and she hadn't answered, sure that it was

Dennis trying to call. But the incessant ringing was getting on her nerves, and this time she snatched up the receiver, prepared to tell Dennis in no uncertain terms not to call anymore.

When she recognized Jordan's voice, she leaned weakly against the counter and closed her eyes. Why had she answered? What was she going to say now?

"I've been trying to get hold of you all afternoon," Jordan said abruptly.

"I was . . . out," Kendall answered, wondering why she was making excuses. "I didn't hear the phone."

"Well, in view of the . . . circumstances, I was wondering if you still want me to have those horses delivered to your place."

Kendall closed her eyes again. She should say no, she told herself. In fact, she should tell him to move the mares he already had here. But the words stuck in her throat. Why couldn't she just tell him and get it over with?

"I would appreciate it if you would keep them," Jordan said, when Kendall remained silent. "But if you've decided against it . . ."

"No," Kendall said faintly. What *was* it about him? she wondered miserably. Even the sound of his voice seemed to render her completely helpless.

"Look, Kendall, I'm sorry about what happened today," he said, and stopped. "I—oh, hell, it seems like all I do lately is apologize for something or other. Maybe we'd better forget the whole thing."

Now was her chance. She should tell him that he was right, that she agreed completely. It *was* better to forget the whole thing; they'd both be happier that way.

Instead, to her horror, she said, "I'm the one who should apologize. Dennis's behavior was . . . inexcusable."

"That wasn't your fault," Jordan said roughly. "I just didn't realize that you and he were—"

"There's nothing between Dennis and me!" Kendall blurted hastily, then cringed. Why was she so eager to assure him of that? Was it because she had detected a faint note of jealousy in his voice? Her heart leaped at the thought, but she suppressed the feeling ruthlessly. She had to be mistaken again, she told herself. It was absurd to think that Jordan might be jealous, especially of Dennis.

"Well, maybe you'd better tell him that. He seems to think—"

"I don't care what he thinks!" Kendall interrupted. "And if you don't mind, I'd rather not talk about it!"

"I'd rather not talk about it either," Jordan said grimly. "In fact, I'd like to forget the whole thing." He hesitated again. "I . . . I didn't handle myself very well today. I was too angry. I'm sorry, Kendall. Maybe we can start over."

Kendall felt like taking the receiver from her ear and staring at it in complete astonishment. Had she heard him right? She couldn't believe it. "I didn't handle myself very well either," she said, surprised into her confession by the one he had made. "Dennis can be so infuriating."

"Yes," Jordan agreed dryly.

It was Kendall's turn to hesitate. She still wasn't sure she was doing the right thing, but then she thought of that young stallion again and how perfect he would be for Jordan's breeding program, and she decided she had to tell him. She knew he had to decide quickly; someone else was sure to see what a prospect the colt was and make an offer if he didn't. So before she could change her mind, she said in a rush, "There's something I wanted to talk to you about."

When she had told him about the colt, Jordan was silent for a moment. "I hadn't planned on buying a stallion for a while," he said finally. "But if you think this is such a good opportunity . . ."

"I do."

"All right," he said decisively. "We'll go take a look at him."

She was dismayed at that. "We?"

He sounded amused. "You don't think I'm going to buy a horse like that without your looking at him, do you? Besides, as I recall, you said today that you'd changed your mind about resigning as my agent. Remember?"

How could she forget? "But I hadn't planned . . . I mean, I can't go."

"Why not?"

"Because . . . because . . ." She couldn't think of an excuse. The thought of going anywhere with him had her so flustered that she couldn't think at all.

"You must have someone you can trust to take care of your place while you're gone," Jordan said. "I'm sure you've had to leave it before, for shows or sales or something."

"Well, of course, but—"

"Well, then?"

Trapped by her own admission, Kendall couldn't think of any more excuses. She never should have told him, she thought wildly. She didn't want to go to Idaho with him. She knew what would happen if she did, and she wasn't ready for that. She had been so determined not to get involved again, and now . . .

"Do you want to call the people to tell them we're coming?" Jordan asked innocently. "Or should I?"

Chapter 8

THE TWO-YEAR-OLD COLT PRANCED ALONG THE PASTURE
fence, silvery tail high, ears cocked forward, the perfect
picture of powerful grace and elegance. The owners,
Bob and Dot Allenby, stood silently by as Kendall and
Jordan watched the horse, but Kendall had seen the
sadness in their eyes, and she sympathized. Because
they were acquaintances of hers, they had confessed
when she called that they were selling out for health
reasons. Bob had suffered a heart attack, and the
doctor had told him the ranch was too much for him
now. The colt was the culmination of their breeding
program, and Kendall knew how difficult it was for
them to give him up. The only consolation was that if
Jordan decided to buy, he would give them a fair price
and the colt a good home.

"What do you think?" Jordan asked quietly, elbows

on the rail, his eyes following the movements of the colt.

"He's a beautiful animal," Kendall said, judging the horse with a practiced eye.

"Do you think I should buy him?"

She didn't hesitate. "Yes."

Jordan nodded. Turning to the Allenbys, he held out his hand and said, "You've just sold your horse."

Bob forced a smile as he shook Jordan's hand. "You've got yourself one fine colt, Mr. Craig. Why don't we go inside out of this cold and settle the deal?"

Jordan didn't haggle about the price. Over coffee and Dot's freshly baked cookies, he told the couple that he didn't want terms. They'd have a cashier's check as soon as he could arrange it with the bank.

"I'll make arrangements for transport as soon as possible," he told them as he and Kendall left. "And don't worry," he added, smiling at the tearful Mrs. Allenby. "He'll have the best of care. I promise."

Dot Allenby nodded, too overcome to speak, and as they drove away, Kendall said quietly, "That was a nice thing you did back there."

Jordan glanced across at her, surprised. "What? Buying the colt, you mean?"

"No. Telling them that you'd take good care of him." She looked at him curiously. "Why did you say that?"

He glanced away again, and she saw by his slight flush that she had embarrassed him. "I could see how fond they were of the horse," he answered. "I knew they didn't want to sell him."

The Allenbys hadn't mentioned their predicament to Jordan, Kendall was sure. For all he knew, this was just another sale to them—a reluctant one, but business all the same. "How did you know?"

"I saw it in their eyes," Jordan replied.

Kendall sat there thoughtfully. He was continually surprising her, she reflected. If it had been Kaylene, she would have offered a lower price—which Kendall was sure the Allenbys would have taken—and then she would have gloated all the way home over the bargain she had gotten.

But Jordan wasn't gloating. In fact, he looked almost sad himself. "You're not sorry you bought the horse, are you?"

He shook his head. "No. I'm just sorry they had to sell it."

She was quiet after that, thinking not so much about what he had said but the way he had said it. He really was a remarkable man, she mused. So complex. Every time she thought she had him figured out, she realized that she didn't have the key at all.

"It looks like we're heading into a storm," Jordan commented.

Kendall looked up through the windshield. She'd been staring out the window without really seeing anything, deep in thought about Jordan. Now she realized that the morning's cloud layer had intensified, and that the sky was an ominous dirty white. The Idaho weather, always so different from that back home, was about to take a turn for the worse. "Do you think it's going to snow?"

"It sure looks that way," he said dryly. "Try to find a weather report on the radio, will you?"

By chance, she turned the dial just as a newscast was concluding. She and Jordan glanced at each other as a resigned voice announced the upcoming blizzard conditions, but even as Kendall said, "I hope he's kidding," the first flakes began to fall. By the time they reached town, the snow was coming down so thick and fast that visibility was almost zero, and Jordan drove directly to the old hotel they had seen on the way out.

The desk clerk greeted them with a cheery, "Looks like we're going to be snowed in for a few days. Hope you folks aren't in a hurry, because nobody's going anywhere in this!"

Kendall was dismayed. "But surely the airport . . ."

The clerk shook his head. "No plane's going to fly in this, ma'am. I'm afraid you'll just have to make the best of it."

Kendall looked at Jordan, sure that he was going to be as upset about the delay as she was. To her surprise, he was smiling.

"I hope you ski," he said. "Because it looks like that's all we'll be doing for the next few days."

"Ski?" Kendall said weakly. "I've never tried it in my life."

"Well, now's a good time to learn," Jordan said, his eyes twinkling. "We can talk about it over dinner."

Dinner was several hours away. When Jordan left her at the door to her room with the excuse that she looked a little tired, promising to meet her downstairs later, Kendall went inside gratefully and immediately smiled with pleasure. The hotel was an old one, and the room reminded her of her own at home, with its flowered wallpaper and hardwood floors decorated with old-fashioned throw rugs. There was even a handmade quilt folded at the foot of the four-poster bed, and she wrapped it around her as she went to the window.

The snow was falling steadily, blanketing the street in pristine white, already piling up on the windowsill.

Kendall was fascinated by the sight; born and raised in
Arizona, she had rarely encountered snow except on
infrequent visits to out-of-state ranches.

There was a rocking chair by the window, and she sat
in it, curling up under the warmth of the quilt, watching
the snowfall and wondering if Jordan was watching it
too. It was curious that he hadn't seemed to mind the
delay, even though neither of them had planned on
staying more than just the day. This was supposed to be
a quick trip to look at a horse, she thought, then home
again and back to their separate lives. Now they were
stranded here for who knew how long, and she wasn't
sure how she felt about that.

The idea of being in his company for several days, so
far from home, filled her with an uneasy mixture of
apprehension and delight, and as she thought about it,
her rocking motions slowed, and then grew still. She
had managed to maintain her distance all day, forcing
herself to be businesslike, deliberately avoiding conver-
sations about anything personal. They had talked about
horses and inconsequential things, and she had been
proud of herself for her control.

But she had been achingly aware of him the entire
time, admiring despite herself the casual way he handled himself in any situation. She had seen the envious
glances that had followed him at the airport and on the
plane; she hadn't missed the fact that the stewardess
had paid special attention to him. Even the girl at the
car rental place had stammered and stuttered, and yet
Jordan had seemed unaware of it all.

He had been brisk and businesslike, too; he hadn't
even touched her, except once when he took her elbow
as they crossed the busy fairway at the airport. Once or
twice she had caught him looking at her, but when she

met his eyes, she couldn't detect anything in his expression.

Well, that was the way she wanted it, wasn't it? She was the one who had insisted on a business relationship and nothing more. Why was she suddenly so resentful that he had taken her at her word?

It was better this way, Kendall assured herself unhappily, watching the snow deepen. Especially now, when they seemed to be trapped here for a few days. If she could just keep her distance, everything would be all right. . . .

She woke with a start in the darkened room, wondering where she was. Disoriented, she sat up, but when the rocking chair creaked gently under her she relaxed again, remembering that she was in a hotel room in a small town in Idaho. Bolting upright again, she also remembered that she was supposed to meet Jordan for dinner, and she hadn't the faintest idea what time it was. Recalling that she had seen a clock on the bedside table, she turned on the lamp and was dismayed to realize that she had slept almost two hours. She had only fifteen minutes before she had to be downstairs, and as she threw off the quilt and rushed into the shower, she wondered what she was going to wear. Then she was impatient with herself. What did it matter what she wore? This was a business trip, she reminded herself; it wasn't an . . . an assignation. The slacks and sweater she had thrown in an overnight bag would just have to do.

Jordan was in the bar when Kendall rushed downstairs twenty minutes later. She saw him sitting there when she paused in the doorway to catch her breath, and for a second or two she just watched him, unable to believe that he was waiting for her. He was so handsome, she thought; she could more easily imagine him waiting for another woman—an elegant creature who would glide gracefully across the room with all eyes following her, everyone thinking what a perfect couple they made when she joined him. The image was so strong in her mind that, for an instant after Jordan turned and smiled at her, Kendall almost expected the fantasy woman to brush by her. She could even smell the woman's perfume, a clinging musky scent carefully calculated to arouse.

Then Jordan stood and came over to her, and the image dissolved. "Are you feeling all right?" he asked.

"Yes, of course. Why?"

"You looked so . . . strange . . . for a moment. As if you'd seen the proverbial ghost."

She forced a laugh. In a way, she had. "I slept too long, I guess," she confessed. "One minute I was sitting in the rocking chair watching the snowfall; the next it was two hours later. I'm sorry I'm late."

"I just got here myself. The same thing happened to me."

This time her laugh was genuine. "Maybe it's the altitude," she said. "Or the excitement. It's not every day you buy a stallion that will be a foundation for your breeding program."

Jordan waited until they were seated and he'd ordered the wine before he responded to her comment. "Is that what you think he'll be?"

"If he breeds up to his potential," Kendall answered honestly. "Yes."

"But a lot of them don't."

"True. But this colt has the bloodlines—and he's an outstanding individual in his own right, as well."

"I really appreciate your help, Kendall. I don't know what I'd do without you."

Kendall flushed, pleased at the compliment, but embarrassed by it, too. "You did just fine with those first mares of yours," she said lightly.

"I told you that was a fluke."

"All beginners should be so lucky!"

The wine came then, and for the next several minutes, while they were giving their order, Kendall was aware of Jordan's eyes on her. For some reason his scrutiny didn't make her as nervous as it usually did; she felt relaxed, almost carefree tonight. All her problems had been left behind in Arizona, and until the storm ended and they could leave again, that was where they would stay. For the first time in months she felt lighthearted and gay, and it was a wonderful feeling. She intended to savor it. Who knew how long it would be before she felt this way again?

"You look happy tonight," Jordan said later, when they had finished their meal.

Kendall smiled. "Do I? Perhaps that's because I don't have any stalls to clean, or horses to feed, or chores to do. Someone else is responsible for all that until we get back, and until then I intend to enjoy the freedom."

"Then you don't mind having to stay here?"

She wanted to say that, as far as she was concerned, it could snow forever. "Oh, no! This hotel is a wonderful old place."

He sat back, studying her. "That's not what I meant."

Kendall suddenly wasn't sure that she wanted to know what he *had* meant. "You mean because of the storm?" she said lightly. "Well, we can't do anything about that, can we?"

He smiled. "I'm glad you feel that way. I thought you'd be impatient about it."

"Not over something like that. Over things I can change, yes." She laughed ruefully. "Patience has never been one of my strong points, I'm afraid."

"I hadn't noticed," he said dryly.

"Oh, I know I hide it so well," she said teasingly. "I never could understand why my father used to tell me never to play poker."

"Tell me about your father. He sounds like a remarkable man."

"He was," she answered, suddenly sounding a little wistful. "Even now, I miss him so much sometimes. . . ."

"If you'd rather not talk about it . . ."

"Oh, no. Talking about him seems to make him closer, somehow. He was always so wise . . . so practical. That's why we were such a good team, I guess. I'd come up with all these wild schemes, and he'd sit there and calmly tell me why most of them wouldn't work. He was the realist, and I was the dreamer, I'm afraid."

"That's hard to believe."

"Why?"

"Because I would have thought it was the other way around. I think you're one of the most practical people I've ever met."

"That's because you didn't know me before," Kendall said, laughing.

"Don't tell me there's still an impractical streak under that solemn exterior," Jordan teased. "I thought all you did was work."

"I'm not working now," she pointed out with a smile.

On impulse, he reached out and covered her hand with his. "I've never seen you like this," he said, suddenly serious. "You're like a different person here."

"So are you," she dared.

His hand still covered hers. "Oh? How is that?"

Kendall was acutely aware of the warmth of his hand, of the slight pressure of his fingers over hers. Fighting the impulse to turn her palm up and lace her fingers through his, she tried to take a deep breath and tell herself this wasn't happening. But as she gazed at him over the flickering of the candle on the table, she saw how dark his eyes were, and how intent, and she knew what he was thinking. Her breath caught again with anticipation, and she felt bold enough to say, "You seem so relaxed tonight, not as—tense as you sometimes are."

It was true, Jordan thought. He hadn't felt this way in longer than he cared to remember. Watching Kendall across the table from him, he was struck anew by how beautiful she was, and it was only by a fierce effort of will that he left his hand where it was. Her hair looked so soft in the candlelight that he wanted to reach out and feel its rich texture under his fingers. He wanted to trace the contours of her face, to touch her soft lips with his own. Her normally expressive eyes seemed even more so tonight, her slender body more pliant. Picturing that delicate body molded to his, he closed his eyes briefly. When he opened them again, she was gazing at him with an expression he couldn't misinterpret. Slowly, almost afraid to move lest he break the spell, he stood up, drawing her up with him.

"Why don't we have an after-dinner drink in the bar?" he asked hoarsely, barely able to speak. He didn't want a drink in the bar; he wanted to sweep her up in his arms and carry her upstairs. But he didn't want to ruin the moment by rushing her; he had waited too long.

Kendall smiled that wonderful smile of hers that he saw so infrequently and that made him feel so weak. "Why don't we have it upstairs?" she whispered.

His fingers tightened on hers. Searching her face, he asked, "Are you sure?"

For an answer, she smiled again and began moving toward the exit. His eyes never leaving her, Jordan pulled some bills from his wallet. Without looking to see what they were, he dropped them on the table. He caught up with her at the doorway, and they went upstairs together.

His room was filled with a soft, silvery glow when they entered, the effect of moonlight on snow. Jordan had left the drapes open, and the scene outside the window was a magical sight: a huge open meadow surrounded by snow-laden trees; a frozen pond glinting under the moon. It had stopped snowing for the moment, but while the clouds were gathering again for another onslaught, the world outside had a breathless quality. There was no sound, and the expanse of meadow was unbroken under its mantle of untrampeled snow. Kendall was enchanted by the sight.

"It's so beautiful," she murmured as Jordan joined her at the window.

He came up behind her, his hands resting lightly on her waist. Feeling breathless herself, she leaned against him, her head on his shoulder, thinking of how long she had anticipated a moment like this and how sure she had been that it would never happen. She could hardly believe it now; the scene outside lent such a dreamlike

quality to the atmosphere that Kendall couldn't be sure
she wasn't dreaming it all herself.

But the pressure of Jordan's hands on her waist was
real, and so were the lips he buried in her hair. She
wanted to turn around and face him, but the moment
was so perfect that she didn't want to end it. They stood
there together, both of them content to gaze silently at
the pristine scene outside, sharing the peaceful sight.
Then, as they watched, a deer emerged tentatively
from the shadow of the trees, walking with delicate
grace through the snow.

"Oh, look!" Kendall said, enthralled.

As if it had heard her, the deer froze in position and
lifted its head, seeming to stare directly at the window
where they were standing. It stood there, absolutely
motionless for a second or two; then, as if sensing some
danger only it could see, it burst into motion, bounding
gracefully away. It was gone in an instant, leaving
behind no sign of its presence except a faint line of
prints in the snow. Kendall sighed with pleasure; it had
been a rare sight, a living postcard to treasure.

Jordan bent his head again, burying his mouth in her
hair, holding her tightly against him. Kendall leaned
into the curve of his body, savoring the moment,
feeling the warmth and strength of his body, all her
senses heightened by the anticipation of what was to
come. When he turned her gently to face him, she
looked up into his eyes, her lips parted, raising her
mouth to his.

They kissed, softly at first, reveling in the pleasure of
gentle contact. But then Kendall felt the trembling of
his arms, and she pressed closer to him, suddenly
wanting—needing—more. It had been so long since she
had been loved by a man; she felt desire welling up in

her like a spring freed from the clutches of winter, like that pond outside warming to the sun. Winding her arms about his neck, she strained to hold him even closer to her.

Jordan put his hand on her breast, uttering a helpless sound as he felt the softness of her flesh. Kendall thrilled to that sound, and when he slipped his hand under her sweater, she was overcome with the desire to strip all their clothes away so that they could be naked in each other's arms. She felt his excitement rising too, and the stream of feeling became a river in her, a flood that burst its banks when he swept her up and carried her over to the rug in front of the fireplace.

He had already touched a match to the logs in the grate when they had first come in; the flames were leaping now, casting shadows over the room, lighting the shadows and hollows of their bodies as they slowly undressed each other.

Jordan's breath caught as he looked at her. "I knew you would be beautiful," he whispered, and bent his head to kiss her throat.

She smiled, tracing the contours of his broad shoulders, placing her hand against the hard muscles of his chest as they lay side by side on the fur rug. Running her eyes down the length of his body, she laughed softly and murmured, "I knew you would be, too."

Jordan pulled a quilt from the couch, wrapping it around them so that they were huddled together inside the soft down. The flickering light shone on his face as he raised himself on one elbow to look at her, and to Kendall his eyes seemed to burn no less intensely than the flames from the grate. Thrilling to the sight, she surrendered to the sensation of lying next to him, luxuriating in the tingling contact of her skin against his. She moved even closer to him, sighing again. Was this really happening? she wondered. She thought that she had never had such a wonderful dream.

Then Jordan kissed her again, and as Kendall reached up for him, the quilt fell away. Neither of them noticed. Kendall felt only the heat of his hands on her, and her own fire leaped within her as he began to caress her. His hands were on her breasts, his thumbs moving over her erect nipples, his head bending to take them in his mouth, his tongue circling until she gasped with the exquisite agony of it and tried to lift his head to hers. The pleasure and the pain and the passion were almost unbearable; she felt consumed by it, every nerve screaming for release, every sense demanding more.

Feverishly, hardly aware of what she was doing, she ran her own hands over his body, closing her eyes against the sudden swift spasm of desire that raced through her at the feel of his trembling legs and his flat stomach and firm buttocks. Reaching down, she held him in her hand, wrapping her legs around him, pulling him toward her. She wanted to feel all of him against her; she wanted to touch every inch of that hard, long body, now straining with a pulsating passion that matched her own. Moaning as his mouth fastened on her breast again, she welcomed him into her.

They began to move as one, she answering each thrust with a movement of her own, raising her hips, drawing him deeper and deeper inside her with every motion. She felt the sheer power of his body drive into her, and she knew she couldn't bear the denial any longer; his mouth and his lips and his tongue had fired her into pure passion, and she pulled his head up, seeking his mouth hungrily, straining to him, willing him to come with her, holding him tightly to her as they were both swept away. She cried out without knowing it, her nails raking his back, her body taut underneath him as he cried out too. They held each other, straining to hold on to that blissful, exquisite, agonizing joy, and in the fireplace, a log snapped, sending up a shower of sparks they neither saw nor heard.

Chapter 9

KENDALL WOKE THE NEXT MORNING TO THE SMELL OF fresh coffee and the tantalizing aroma of home-baked biscuits. She opened her eyes to see Jordan sitting on the side of the bed, and when she smiled sleepily at him, he said teasingly, "I thought you were going to sleep all day!"

Kendall stretched luxuriously under the blankets. "What time is it?"

"Almost ten."

"Ten! I haven't slept that long in years!" She sat up with the blankets still wrapped around her, gratefully accepting the cup of coffee he held out to her. "Where did you get this—and those!" she said, spying the tray of biscuits on the bedside table. "I didn't know they had room service here!"

"They don't." He grinned. "I went down to the kitchen and roused the cook."

Kendall closed her eyes appreciatively. "Breakfast in bed!" she sighed. "What a treat."

"Well, I'm afraid that's all the treat you're going to get today. The roads are impassable; we can't get to a ski area unless we use snowshoes."

Kendall put her cup on the table. "Oh, and I was so looking forward to learning how to ski!" she said with a mock pout.

"Oh, yes, I could tell that by the way you sprang out of bed this morning," Jordan said dryly.

She sighed, looking at him from under her lashes. "Well, I guess we'll just have to think of something else to do then, won't we?"

He smiled. "Do you have any suggestions?"

Grinning wickedly at him, she slid down on the pillows again. "Oh, maybe one or two."

He grinned back at her. "You know, so do I. Would you like to hear what they are?"

"Why don't we compare notes?"

"I think that's an excellent idea," he said solemnly. "Mind if I join you?"

"Be my guest."

Smiling at their nonsense, Kendall watched as he quickly stripped off his clothes, admiring his muscled body, remembering what that body had done to her last night. She felt a return of desire just looking at him, and as he turned to her again, she lifted the edge of the sheet so that he could crawl in beside her.

"Lord! It's cold out here!" he said.

She moved close to him. "Maybe we should start a fire."

He looked down at her. "I think you already have."

She laughed. "I meant in the fireplace."

"And I meant—"

"I know what you meant." She laughed again and nestled closer to him.

Snuggled under the mound of blankets, with his arms around her, Kendall put her head on his shoulder, thinking that if she had her way it would always be like this.

She felt more than physically close to him this morning; there seemed to be a wordless communication beneath their banter, as well, and she sighed again in complete contentment as he stroked her back. The day stretched lazily in front of them, and if they chose, they could spend it all right here. It was snowing again, and as she glanced indolently toward the window she saw frost riming the panes, etching delicate patterns on the glass. She knew it was freezing outside, but lying here next to the warmth of Jordan's body, she felt she would never be cold again.

Jordan's hand moved to her shoulder, and he sighed too. She looked up curiously at him, and he smiled as he dropped a kiss on her nose. "I was just thinking that there's nothing like the feel of a woman's skin," he murmured. "I wonder why that is?"

Kendall reached up to run her fingers over his mouth. "Why does nothing compare to a man's hands on a woman's body?" she asked, returning the smile.

He grinned. "I don't know. But aren't we lucky it works out that way?"

She laughed, an invitation in her eyes. "Maybe we'd better make sure it still does."

"Maybe we'd better," he said seriously, and pulled her over on top of him.

They took more time to explore each other than they

had the night before, delighting in the scent and sensation of each other, touching and caressing and stroking, prolonging the anticipation and the pleasure until they were both trembling.

Kendall marveled at the movement and definition of Jordan's muscles, running her hands down his body, kneading his hard flesh under her fingers. With her eyes closed, she felt how strong his legs were and how flat his belly. His chest was so broad and his shoulders so wide that she felt small and delicate as she lay on top of him, and when his arms went around her she felt safe and protected, as if nothing could happen to her as long as she stayed within the powerful circle of his embrace.

Jordan felt a sense of wonder at how tiny she seemed beside him. She was so slender that she felt like a feather, her bones so small and fine that he was almost afraid he might crush her. And yet he delighted at the petite strength he felt in her lithe body, feeling how firm her flesh was, and how smooth. He laughed softly when he discovered that he could almost encircle her waist with his hands, and the feel of her breasts in his cupped hands filled him with even greater desire. She was so beautiful, he thought, and he told her so, his breath catching in his throat as he gazed up at her.

Kendall's eyes seemed very green as she gazed back at him. Then, very slowly, she lowered her head, just touching his lips with her own. The gesture sent a spasm throughout his entire body, and without his volition, his arms tightened around her again. They rolled back and forth on the tumbled bed, his hands seeking now with greater urgency, his mouth hungry on hers.

Kendall responded with the same intensity of passion. As slowly as they had caressed each other before, they moved quickly together now, bodies suddenly demanding release from the tension that had been building without their being fully aware of it. Like the match Jordan had set to the dry kindling last night, their desire became a fire; it raced through them both, sweeping them along in its path. They reached the heights together, entwined in a fierce embrace, arms and legs and bodies melded into one as the last shuddering paroxysm took them away. Still locked together, they looked into each other's eyes at that final exultant moment. Laughing with complete abandon, they clung to each other long after the last shuddering spasm drifted slowly away, and Kendall thought that she had never been so happy, so utterly, completely content.

They went for a walk that afternoon, Kendall insisting on braving the snow and the deep drifts in the meadow because she was determined to see the frozen pond.

It was cold outside, and she breathed deeply of the crisp air, watching her breath escape in clouds of vapor, feeling exhilarated as they struggled through the snow. She didn't notice for a few minutes that Jordan had fallen behind; she was too caught up in the beauty of the meadow, where the only tracks were their own, and the boughs of the pines drooped under their burden of fluffy white. Even the tracks of the deer they had seen the night before had been obliterated by the fresh snowfall; it was as if they were the first to enter the meadow, claiming it by right of discovery.

Then she realized that Jordan wasn't with her. She

turned to him with a teasing remark on her lips and
stopped, frozen by his expression as he stood some
distance behind her.

He looked as if he were in the grip of some awful
pain. His face was as white as the snow, and he stood
stiffly, as if commanding the spasm, or whatever it was,
to abate by sheer force of will. Terrified, she hurried
back to him, struggling through the deep drifts, half
falling in her haste.

"What is it?" she cried when she finally reached him.
"Jordan, what's wrong?"

"It's . . . nothing," he said through clenched teeth.
"Just give me a minute . . . it will pass."

"But what is it?" she asked shrilly, alarmed by the
obvious effort he made to speak. She saw the drops of
sweat on his forehead, and she was even more fright-
ened. "I'm going for help," she said, and started away.

His hand shot out, stopping her with such a fierce
grip that she winced. "I . . . said . . . it . . . will . . .
pass."

"But—"

"Leave it, will you?" he said savagely, struggling for
breath.

So she was forced to stand by silently, watching him
and pretending not to, until finally that terrifying
stiffness left him and he was able to breathe normally
again. After what seemed an endless time, he brushed
his sleeve across his forehead and muttered, "I'm
sorry."

"You don't have to be *sorry!*" she cried, still beside
herself with concern. "What was it? Why won't you tell
me what's wrong?"

He shook his head as if to clear his mind. "I told
you—it was nothing."

The curt finality of his tone silenced her again, but as they walked slowly back to the hotel, she couldn't prevent herself from watching him covertly. He was still pale, although at least his face had lost that ghastly grayish tone. But he walked as if he were still in pain, and her worry increased. She wanted to insist that he see a doctor, but she knew it would be a useless plea, when he had insisted that nothing was wrong, so she made herself be silent. She didn't even dare try to help him up the stairs when they finally got back to the hotel; she went ahead of him, wondering if she should accompany him to his room or if she should just go along to hers and leave him alone.

"Jordan, if there's anything I can do . . . ," she began hesitantly when they reached her door.

He shook his head. "I told you, it was nothing to be concerned about," he said impatiently. "A muscle spasm, that's all. The famous charley horse. Let's not make a big deal of it, all right?"

She made herself nod in agreement, knowing that it had been much more than a simple muscle spasm, but unable to find the words that would bring him back to her. She could feel him slipping away behind that wall of his, and she knew with despair that there was nothing she could do about it. "If that's the way you want it," she said quietly.

"It is. Look, I'll meet you for dinner."

She shook her head. "I think I'll skip dinner," she said. "I'm not really hungry tonight."

"Kendall . . ."

"It's all right, Jordan," she said quickly, trying not to cry. "I'm just tired, I guess. I'll see you in the morning."

He didn't argue. With a brief nod, he went to his own

room down the hall. Kendall waited until he had gone inside, hoping until the last that he would turn around and at least look at her, but when he shut the door with finality, she had to will herself to stay where she was. She wanted to run after him, to beg him to tell her what had happened, to assure him that whatever it was, she would help in any way she could. But she knew the utter futility of that now, and her steps dragged as she entered her own room.

With her eyes blurred with tears, she went to the window and looked out at the meadow. She could see the tracks they had made in the snow, but suddenly it wasn't beautiful anymore. It looked as cold and empty and bleak as she felt inside, and she turned away. As she did, the clouds parted momentarily, and a weak ray of late-afternoon sun shone through. The storm was finally passing. By morning the roads would be clear and they would be free to leave. By the time they got home it would seem as if the past two days had never happened.

And maybe they never had, she thought as she threw herself down despondently on the bed. Maybe she had just dreamed the whole thing. It was obvious that what had been a magical time for her had only been a diversion for him, she thought miserably. As much as it hurt her to admit it, she knew that it was true. If it wasn't, Jordan wouldn't have shut her out like that; he would have confided in her, told her what was wrong. They would have faced it together; he would have allowed her to help in some way.

But he hadn't wanted to confide in her; he had withdrawn, retreated behind that impenetrable wall he used to hold her at arm's length, and that hurt most of all. She had believed they shared more than physical desire; she had hoped that this would lead to something more—that their relationship would develop in all ways.

She had been wrong, it seemed, so wrong. Jordan didn't want a relationship at all; he wanted an uncomplicated affair—a physical thing, with no emotional commitments on either side. She had been a fool to think otherwise, and she cringed now at the thought of how easily she had surrendered to him.

She had deliberately abandoned herself to her desire for him, thrusting away any thought of consequences, knowing the danger of involvement with such an intensely private, complex man, and not caring, not even admitting the possibility that she might be hurt. She had wanted more—much more—than he was willing to give, and now she was paying for it.

He hadn't made any promises, she reminded herself. She was the one who had romanticized the affair, and the humiliation she felt at the thought was so overwhelming that she couldn't even cry. She lay there, staring dry-eyed up at the ceiling, not noticing the chill in the room until long past nightfall. Too despondent to start a fire, she finally pulled the quilt over her and huddled inside it, wondering if this misery would ever pass.

Somehow, she doubted it.

Jordan stood at the window in his room, gazing down at the meadow and picturing Kendall there, her eyes sparkling, her face rosy from the cold. Even under the thick parka she had worn, she'd looked slender and graceful, like the deer they had seen last night. She was

so beautiful, he thought, closing his eyes in pain. So
vulnerable. He had hurt her just now; he had seen it in
her face—the worry and concern clouding her expressive eyes, the slight trembling of the mouth that he
loved to kiss. Her lips were so soft, he thought, and
abruptly he turned away from the window.

He lit a cigarette and threw himself into a chair,
brooding about what had happened. The ache in his
back immediately set up a clamor, but he almost
welcomed the pain; it seemed a just punishment after
the way he had treated Kendall. There were some pills
in his shaving kit for occasions like this, but he refused
to take them. He wanted to feel the pain; maybe then
he could occupy himself with fighting that, instead of
thinking about what a fool he had been.

Why hadn't he just told her about the back problem?
he asked himself angrily. It would have been so simple;
she certainly would have understood. She'd *wanted* to
understand. She had begged him for an explanation.
He had scared her to death acting that way, and for
what purpose? He was always angry when he had these
spasms; they seemed such a betrayal by his own body.
He'd been told that eventually they'd go away entirely,
that he should just take the pills when he needed them.
It was an aftereffect; you couldn't break your back and
not have some residual damage—or so the doctor had
assured him. He'd made remarkable progress as it was,
they told him. No one had expected him to walk again
after the accident, so a few muscle spasms were a small
price to pay for recovery. He should be grateful that he
had survived at all.

Survived. That was an apt word, he thought with a
bitter twist of his lips. That was all he'd been doing—

surviving, existing, enduring . . . until he met Kendall. She had revived something in him that he'd thought long dead, and he hadn't wanted to admit it. The past two days with her had been a revelation; she had opened his eyes to all he was missing—all he *had* missed in a relationship with a woman—and the intensity of his feelings for her scared him. It was more than a physical experience; he had found himself watching her when she wasn't looking, loving the way she walked or talked or gestured. He wanted to share his thoughts with her, his hopes and dreams as well as his nightmares; he wanted to hear those things from her, and yet . . .

Yet he had used the experience in the meadow just now to thrust her away. He had seized it as the perfect excuse to put up a barrier between them. He was becoming too involved, too close to her . . . too near to asking her to share his life, and that scared him most of all.

He wasn't ready for that, not after his marriage to Marie. He felt he had failed his wife in so many ways. He just hadn't seemed capable of giving her what she wanted emotionally, and he wasn't going to make the same mistake where Kendall was concerned.

But Kendall wasn't Marie, a small voice inside his head pointed out. Marie had been helpless, clinging to him, looking to him for support he just couldn't give—not all the time, anyway. Kendall was strong, independent; she knew what she wanted and was determined to get it. She didn't want—or need—to lean on a man; she would never make the demands on him that Marie unconsciously had. Kendall really didn't need him at all, and maybe that was what bothered him the most.

What did he want? Jordan asked himself angrily. He'd just told himself that he couldn't handle another clinging woman like Marie, but perversely, he wished Kendall needed him more.

He didn't know what he wanted, that was the problem. And that was why he had used that incident in the meadow as an excuse. He needed time to think. He had to decide what it was that he really did want.

Except now he probably wouldn't get the chance to decide anything at all. After the way he'd treated Kendall just now, he wouldn't blame her if she never spoke to him again. Dismayed at the thought, he was halfway out of his chair before he made himself sit back again.

He had to give them both time to work things out, he thought. As much as he wanted to straighten out this mess he had made of everything, he couldn't go back to her right now and tell her that he'd been a fool. He couldn't explain how confused he felt, how uncertain, when he couldn't even explain those things to himself.

Depressed and angry with himself, Jordan lit another cigarette. Deep in thought, he didn't notice the one still burning in the ashtray by his hand.

Kendall didn't see or hear from Jordan for several days after the return trip from Idaho. The plane ride home had been a nightmare, both of them acting like strangers instead of the passionate lovers they had been, the distance between them growing with every mile. By the time the plane landed, Kendall was so taut from nerves that she felt like bursting into tears. As Jordan drove swiftly home, she sat silently on her side